AUSTIN DUFFY is the autho[r]
and Immortal Thing, which
Group Irish Novel of the Yea[r]
McKitterick Prize. He is a prac[tising]
lives in Ireland with his wife and two children.

'Stylish, mordant, and pitch-perfect – I read it in one sitting. If Rachel Cusk or Sally Rooney had been junior doctors they might have come up with something like this' Gavin Francis

'*The Night Interns* is an utterly immersive read. Duffy has managed to capture the claustrophobia, exhaustion and constant pressure of life in a contemporary hospital so effectively I could physically feel the tension on every page. A gripping, honest and incredibly important book' Jan Carson

'Entirely gripping, like *Squid Game* for medical students. *The Night Interns* exposes a fascinating but terrifying backstage glimpse of an apparently functioning hospital where the director is a tyrant, the producer is unhinged, and the actors don't know their lines. It is highly unusual that a person who has access to knowledge as specialised as this – the mechanics of life and death – is also gifted with an artist's sensibility. This novel is to be prized on so many levels' Claire Kilroy

'As well as being a critically acclaimed author, Austin Duffy is a medical oncologist, so it's no surprise that this slight but effective sketch of surgical interns struggling through the bleak, brutal hours of the night shift seems so authentic... There are moments of *This Is Going To Hurt*-style black comedy' *Daily Mail*

'[Austin Duffy] shares Chekhov's close-quarters awareness of the demands, anxieties and hard-won value of a doctor's life and his ability to convey it with unillusioned honesty and unsentimental poignancy... Duffy unfolds not just the challenges [the interns] face, but also the warren-like institution within which they work...A terrific feat of immersive writing...Character sketches – a bullying near-retirement surgeon, a bumptious registrar, status skirmishes between nurses and interns – vividly and sometimes comically display the prickly hierarchies inside the tense workplace...Alive with the immediacy of first-hand observation, the novel can modulate from sardonic wit to moments of heart-wrenching affectingness' *Sunday Times*

'The dreaded night shift is by turns frenetic, monotonous, stressful, endless. Through Duffy's skilled depiction, the hospital emerges as a harsh world of ugly paradoxes...This book will cement [Duffy's] reputation as an astute chronicler of the medical world and the difficult lives of its practitioners... *The Night Interns* is a disconcerting and exacting record of what goes on behind the scenes at a busy Irish hospital. Engrossing' *Irish Times*

'There is a tremendous tension in the spheres in which the characters move, prosaic diffidence and mania often graduating to near hallucinatory episodes of transfiguration... [Duffy] uses eeriness, tact and even bleak humour to reconcile us to deadening facts' *Irish Examiner*

'The reader ends up marked by the reading experience, holding the paperback, finished and closed, unwilling to immediately rejoin the real world...Austin Duffy is currently a full-time medical consultant. Readers must hope he continues to find enough time to continue to produce a jewelled novel every couple of years' *Irish Examiner*

'Duffy writes with the economy, style and quiet authority that marks him out as one of the most exciting voices in contemporary Irish fiction' *Sunday Business Post*

The Night Interns

AUSTIN DUFFY

GRANTA

Granta Publications, 12 Addison Avenue, London, W11 4QR

First published in Great Britain by Granta Books, 2022

This paperback edition published by Granta Books, 2023

A CIP catalogue record for this book
is available from the British Library

1   3   5   7   9   10   8   6   4   2

ISBN 978 1 78378 835 4 (paperback)
ISBN 978 1 84708 834 7 (ebook)

www.granta.com

Typeset in Garamond by Patty Rennie
Printed and bound by CPI Group (UK) Ltd, Croydon, CR0 4YY

MIX
Paper | Supporting
responsible forestry
FSC® C171272
www.fsc.org

For my parents, Vincent and Pauline Duffy

He held my hand,
And even smiled, which gave some comfort when
He led me through the gate to a strange land
Where sighs and moans and screams of ruined men,
Filling the air beneath a starless sky,
Resounded everywhere, and everywhere
Was there inside me.

Dante Alighieri, *The Divine Comedy*

HER FACE, WE agreed, could only be described as serene. There were no lines on it. The tightness of pain was gone, her worried eyes were now closed. None of us had wanted to enter the room in the first place. She's cheyne stoking, the nurse told us as we stood outside it. Lynda was annoyed that they had called us at all. I mean, what did they expect us to do about it? She pushed past Stuart and me and opened the door. We had no choice but to follow her into the room. Sure enough the woman's breathing had entered that unnatural rhythm. Up until then we had only read about it, but here it was happening right in front of us, pre-death in all its glory. It was louder than we would have imagined, a slow but very deep grunting, like a beached sea creature drowning in oxygen, not very human, frankly. Even Lynda was taken aback. For a few seconds the three of us stood looking at the woman from the bottom of the bed. Her face was a perfect mask, already far gone, but the chest didn't know it yet and was heaving away of its own accord. It was as if her disguise had been removed, the body stripped to reveal the alien presence at its core, what all along had been propelling it.

The family were spread around the periphery of the room. They were watching us and it felt like we should do something, or at least say something to them, but there we stood, as lost as they were. Finally Lynda stepped forward, uncoiling her stethoscope. She listened to the woman's lungs and looked into her mouth with her pen torch. It was no easy thing to pry open her jaws. Lynda's confidence amazed us. Afterwards we asked her what she had seen and she said nothing of course, just blackness. She said something to the nurse, and then to the woman's family, about trying to make her more comfortable, and they seemed OK with that. It was a relief when somehow the door opened behind us and we backed out of the room, Stuart and I bowing like geishas. Lynda's pager went off and we followed her to the nurses' station while she answered it. The food's here, she said, putting down the phone. The nurses had a few more jobs for us, nothing major, just charting stuff. We did whatever they asked and when we were finished Lynda told them not to call us again unless it was absolutely necessary. We left the ward and headed to the stairwell by Sir Patrick Duns ward that would take us down to the ground floor. From there we would make our way back to the res.

— This is why we need to divide up the night, Lynda said.

She looked at me and then back at Stuart, who had fallen a few steps behind.

— I mean it, she said, there was no need for the three of us to be standing there gawking at that poor woman.

Neither Stuart nor I said anything and Lynda's words were left to hang. The stairwell brought us down two flights and we emerged into the radiology department. It was always so eerie to go through radiology at this hour. The waiting area was completely empty, a grille pulled down over the reception area where the secretaries sat during opening hours. By day, this was the busiest part of the hospital – it constantly thronged with people and was the centre of the hospital's activity. But all that seemed inconceivable now. It was as if we had stumbled upon a lost world whose place in time had long since passed.

— The others all split up the night, Lynda said. They get two hours' sleep guaranteed. Four if only one of them holds the bleeps. Can you imagine that? Four hours! God, you'd be totally fine the next day.

— Yeah, I said, but the rest of the time would be hell.

— So what? Lynda said. If you're going to be up anyway you might as well be working.

We left radiology and turned on to the long link corridor that stretched off into the distance. We could barely make out the far end of it. The corridor spanned the length of the hospital and we used to joke about using roller blades to get up and down it, but such a frivolous thing was unimaginable now. We started on the long trudge, weighed down by our white coats made heavier by the things we carried in their deep pockets – tape, a coiled stethoscope, a reflex hammer – as well as by the handbooks that Stuart and I carried. The BNF, a MIMMS, the *Oxford Handbook of Clinical Medicine*. Stuart also had one on procedures. Lynda used to make fun of us about the books. What are you going to do in an emergency, she'd say, turn to page seventy-nine? Her white coat didn't seem to weigh her down at all. She strode on slightly ahead of us, her back straight, her hands pushed all the way into her empty pockets. As a teenager she had been a champion runner, and you could see this in her gait, the way she walked mainly on her toes, ready to spring at you.

Lynda's pager went off. Its piercing sound reverberated around us. Looking down at the number on the pager, she let out a groan.

– Colles, she said.

– We were only there a while ago, I said.

There was a phone on the wall, but Lynda walked right past it. She thought it was ridiculous that the hospital was still using pagers. Why couldn't they just call us on our mobiles? I saw Stuart looking anxiously at the phone on the wall and then at Lynda as she marched onward, both of us following in her wake. I was fine with her ignoring the call. The only thing I wanted to focus on was making it to the res and having some food. If we didn't eat now we might not get a chance later. Nights were unpredictable like that. The lulls could be as long as an hour or they might not occur at all. It wasn't long before Lynda's pager went off again and we knew even before she checked the number that it would be Colles ward again. The nurses always paged you twice if you didn't answer straight away. Things like that annoyed us, but they drove Lynda crazy. She increased her pace in anger. By now we were at the turn-off for OPD. A receptionist's desk was outside it and Lynda went behind it. As she picked up the phone she stared back at us.

— Why don't they ever call you two? she said.

Again, neither Stuart nor I said anything and her words were left hanging. We avoided eye contact with her. The question wasn't fair as Stuart and I got our share of calls, though perhaps it was true that Lynda got the majority. You would think it would be the opposite given how she spoke to the nurses. She always gave them a grilling when they called her and often was outright rude to them. A few weeks ago one of them made a complaint about her, but even this didn't seem to bother Lynda. Now she stood staring back at us in accusation as she waited for the nurses on Colles to answer the phone. It took them ages, another thing that infuriated us. Another reason why they should call us on our mobiles. When they eventually did pick up we could hear the nurse's voice on the other end but couldn't make out what she was saying. All we heard was Lynda's side of the conversation.

— Well have you given him a fluid bolus? she said ...Why not? ...Yeah, well maybe you could do that and then recheck it ...No, you don't need to call us back if it's OK ...One of us will chart it when we get there ... It's only a fluid bolus for God's sake ... Five hundred mls. Thank you.

She hung up.

— Useless, she said.

When she came out from behind the desk she looked at Stuart and burst out laughing.

— It's OK, Stuart, she said. If they put in a complaint I'll tell them you had nothing to do with it. That you weren't even here. OK?

We went back out on to the link corridor to resume the trek back to the res. If it hadn't been for the security lights outside the windows we would have been in total darkness. They were dotted at overlapping intervals, projecting pools of fake moonlight inwards. We couldn't see out through the blackness of the glass, which only returned our ghostly images back to us. I straightened up when I saw how hunched over I was. All we could hear was the squeak of our runners off the oily surface, the rustle of our scrubs. One of the few consolations of being on call was that we could dress in surgical scrubs despite never being required to go near the operating theatre.

We could even get away with wearing them the next day when we continued into our day jobs, which didn't have anything to do with operating either, because surgical interns didn't do any actual surgery. Our job by day was to take care of the general ward work, the 'scut work', as Sharif, my registrar, described it. Mostly that boiled down to doing whatever odd jobs the nurses needed us to do on behalf of the patients, lines replaced which had tissued, urinary catheters inserted, blood cultures drawn, first dose antibiotics administered, fluids charted, the drug kardexes rewritten. There was very little actual doctoring. But at the same time we were also supposed to be on hand to deal with whatever might happen out of the blue. We were the first people the nurses would call if someone went off, and we were always the first arrivers on the scene. God only knew what situation would be there to greet us when we arrived, and what vacancy in our medical knowledge it would expose. This wasn't much of a concern during the day when there were people around to help, but at night it was a different story. It was clear that Lynda wasn't going to let the matter drop.

– Seriously though, she said, there's absolutely no point in the three of us going around together like this. It's so inefficient!

— Yeah, I said, we should definitely think about it.

— We can do more than that. At some point you have to be able to stand on your own two feet.

She was looking at Stuart, and it was clear that this remark was aimed at him. Lately she couldn't be bothered hiding her frustration with him, the fact that we always had to watch out for him. Lynda thought he was no use. From the beginning of intern year it had seemed we were practically doing his job for him, putting in his lines, or doing his blood gases. He rarely got these things in first time, and he approached them with zero confidence. It was like he had defeated himself before he had even tried, and the patients could sense this, which only made things worse. The problem was that these were the most rudimentary parts of the job. So imagine his fear at being left all alone to cover the entire hospital, even for a few hours.

— There's Ed, I said.

You could see him out the window, a small figure standing in the glare of Hospital 5's security light. He could have been drifting in space as he held on to our food delivery in its plastic bag. The three of us paused to look

9

at him. He was only a hundred yards away, and if the windows hadn't been sealed we could have beckoned him over to us across the no man's land of darkness. But instead he would have to wait another few minutes for us. The hospital was enormous, but in a spread-out rather than built-up way. The corridor would bring us round the long way, through the private wards. Then we would take another link corridor to get to the res at the back of Hospital 5, in the consultant car park.

We turned the corner and Ed fell out of sight. He'd be annoyed that we took so long, but there was nothing we could do about it. We went up the stairwell to the second floor to avoid going through Private 1, which always had a million jobs for us.

— What about the burns unit?

It was the first thing Stuart had said in a while. He'd clearly been mulling things over.

— What about it?

— We'd have to cover that too, right?

Lynda looked at me and I pretended not to follow what he was getting at. She glared at Stuart.

— Half of them have Hickmans in, she said. So you don't even have to worry about taking bloods or putting in lines! Plus the nurses there are at least semi-competent. You'd just have to do what they tell you. For God's sake, it's just charting fluids mostly. You should be able to handle that much on your own!

Stuart looked at the floor. It was doubtful that he'd found any of that reassuring. Lynda looked at me and I gave her the same look back, which hopefully said *I know, I know*, despite the fact that the burns unit was also the first thing I had thought about. I hated going there, especially if it was for a review. The nurses would lead you into one of the rooms, to a patient wrapped in tin foil. You couldn't even make out their features beneath the wrapping and extensive bandaging and tissue damage. They would be lying on beds like inflatable thrones and surrounded by strange machines that were constantly beeping, as if they were trying to tell you what was wrong with the patient but in an alien language that you didn't understand. It was easy for Lynda because she worked in the burns unit during the day, so she knew their ways. She also knew the nurses and even most of the patients, so she was comfortable dealing with them and their particular situation. You would almost go so far as to call it confidence. In practical terms, she also knew which consultants were on and therefore which jobs needed to be done or which ones could be safely deferred until the next day. It was one of the great advantages of having Lynda on our team, the fact that she took it upon herself to deal with the burns unit.

We climbed the back staircase, finding every step a struggle. Lynda's obvious annoyance didn't help. It was an extra burden for me and Stuart to carry. Lately she had been getting more insistent about dividing up the night. She brought it up now every time we were on call, which was one in four, sometimes one in three. The rest of the time we didn't see each other much as we were far too busy with our daytime jobs. Lynda was the plastics intern, while I was attached to Professor Lynch, one of the general surgeons. Stuart was doing ENT and was probably the least busy of the three of us, but you wouldn't guess it if you saw him running about the place during the day as if the world was about to end. But right now our daytime jobs seemed a million miles away, and the hospital itself, or at least its daytime demeanour – so hectic with its packed waiting rooms and busy departments and teams of uniformed workers, doctors, nurses, OTs, physios, dieticians, porters all milling around – seemed inconceivable. It was only the long, empty night that existed for us, stretching out ahead with no end in sight. If you had told me there was a chance that this particular one might never end, I would have believed you. The busy daytime hospital might as well not have existed at all. The way things were right now was the only reality for us, and we were the central protagonists in it, together with the nurses on night duty, who were sometimes allied with us and sometimes our bitter enemies. The only other people who existed for us were the patients, most of whom were sleeping the sleep of the sick, restless and uncomfortable, in various stages of chronic ill health or even beginning their descent through the spiral of death, which is irreversible once it has built up a head of steam. Only some of the patients would be awake and capable of speaking to us, either in pain or in some psychic distress and – God help them – they were the ones who were most dependent upon us. They didn't know that we didn't know anything, and it was probably better that way.

We emerged out of the ground-floor stairwell at the far end of Private 1, stopping at its carpeted border. Lynda held up her hand to tell Stuart and me to wait despite the fact that we knew the drill by now. She poked her head round the corner to make sure none of the nurses were around. Quick, she said, and we scampered across the ward to get to the small link corridor that led to the res. Stuart was last and didn't even seem to be hurrying. A nurse came out of one of the side rooms and saw him. Lynda and I heard her calling out to him and then to one of her colleagues, saying, Joan, Joan, the intern is here, do we need him for anything? Lynda had to go back and step on to the bright carpet. She shouted at the nurse that if it wasn't urgent they should make a list and we'd get to it later.

– It might be urgent, the nurse said. I'll check with Joan.

– If you have to check with Joan then it's not urgent, Lynda said, turning away and taking Stuart with her.

The light was out in the small corridor leading to the res, so it felt like a leap of faith to close the door behind us and enter the tunnel of darkness that joined the res to the hospital. The air changed and was cooler. I was reminded of those passageways in spaceships where you have to close one hatch with a steering wheel to create the vacuum and only then can you open the hatch at the other end. Coming into the res was like returning to a house in darkness. Not that you would call it homely, but it was a safe zone all the same. The corridor was lined by empty single rooms, all their doors closed. Most of the rooms were unoccupied, and earlier on that evening we had had our pick of them when we were getting changed into our scrubs. Without thinking, I had chosen the room nearest the kitchen, but just as I was closing the door I saw Stuart looking at me. I remembered then that it had been Arnie's room the night he made his big jump, so I came out of it and picked a different one. As I passed it now I could see my bag on the floor where I had left it, and we continued along the corridor to the kitchen. The place was freezing, we could see our breath on the air. It disappeared when we turned on the light.

Ed the delivery man was very annoyed that we had taken so long, and who could blame him? It was dark and isolated where he had to wait for us. All he had to protect him was the security light, as if its magic powers would somehow keep him safe from the lowlifes known to loiter in the vicinity with their blood syringes. When it was dark they emerged like the undead from the Oliver Plunkett flats complex that you could see lit up in the distance by floodlights. At night the car park was empty except for the odd forlorn car belonging to someone on call. An SHO had been raped there a few years before, and people were always getting mugged. A Chinese delivery man would be easy pickings, and he let Lynda have it when she went to deal with him. While she was gone it was just me and Stuart there in the res kitchen. We sat at one of the two long tables. Stuart was in a subdued, pensive mood, more than usual. You could almost hear the anxiety crashing in waves against the inside of his skull.

– Don't you think it's fine the way we do things now? he said. I mean, we're going to be changing rotations in a couple of weeks, why change things now?

I shrugged my shoulders as if what Lynda was proposing was no big deal, that personally I could go either way. The truth was, though, that Lynda had a point. The way we did things was extremely inefficient. At the beginning it had been my idea to stick together, but that was only supposed to be for the first few weeks, when none of us knew anything and we could pool whatever small skills we were developing. There was safety in numbers, or at least the illusion of it. If one of us couldn't get an IV in, then one of the others would have a go at it. I'd never catheterized anyone, for example, so Lynda showed me how. And in fairness, Stuart was good at drug doses. He carried three pharmacology handbooks with him, not just the BNF. Even if someone was allergic to multiple antibiotics, he'd be sure to come up with something. So we dovetailed nicely. Beginning early in the evening, we would work our way through the wards systematically and in sequence, starting with the ortho ward, which was always the worst, their patients fine from an ortho-paedic point of view, but a total mess otherwise. That would take up the first few hours, after which we would move on, spending extended periods of time on each ward, not leaving until they had been cleared of their list of jobs which we always asked the nurses to compile in an effort to stop them paging us every time something popped into their heads. You would think the nurses would have preferred it that way too, but not a chance. We took too long to get to them, they said, we were like one of those slow country coaches, they said, the ones which plod their way along, and even though you might see their headlights in the distance, they never seem to arrive. The nurses told us they didn't like it when the three of us were on. One or two of them even threatened to file an incident report about us, which Lynda found hilarious. Oh no, not an incident report, she would say, please, anything but that, and she'd laugh in their faces.

A newspaper was on the table, and I pulled it over to look at it. I felt Stuart's eyes on me and knew he could see through my fake confidence. I felt a flash of irrita-tion. I wouldn't mind, but the pretence was partly for his benefit. From the beginning Lynda and I had taken on the role of constantly reassuring him. Nothing had been said to us directly, but it was understood that we were all to keep an eye on each other, in particular the weaker members in our midst, those who looked like they couldn't handle things. Nobody wanted another Arnie situation. We were supposed to be watching each other like hawks to prevent it happening again. What exactly we were looking out for was never clear. Signs of stress? Trepidation? Inadequacy and the utter fear of God? We had all of these already. But it was generally agreed that some among us were particularly prone. You only had to glance at Stuart to see that he fit the bill. The big worried head on him. He was quite open about the fact that as soon as intern year was done he was heading for the psychiatry scheme.

– Look , I said, it probably wouldn't be too bad. I mean, the reg and SHO are down in casualty, and there will always be two of us back in the res. We'd just be a phone call away. I mean, what's the worst thing that could happen?

He looked even more alarmed. He knew as well as I did that under no circumstances were we to call the reg or SHO in casualty – or at the most, under only a very few

circumstances. A rupture or something, Sharif my registrar had told me at the beginning of the year, when he
found out that he was also the covering surgical reg for
what was our first night on call. I mean it, Sharif had said.
Someone's leg better be hanging off. Maybe an arm. He
laughed, but he was being deadly serious. If it was just a
line that we couldn't get into someone, for antibiotics or
some other nonsense, then we were to keep trying until
we got it, Sharif said. OK? You can try fifty times as far as
I'm concerned. Turn their arm into a pin cushion for all I
care. Sure, we were welcome to call the anaesthetist if we
felt like it, but good luck with that because they were even
less likely to come and help us. Above all, and here Sharif
really meant it, I wasn't to call him with anything that was
vaguely medical, cardiac or any of that blood-sugar nonsense. If I did that, he swore to God that he would reach
down the phone and personally strangle me by the throat.
And by the way, I could forget about getting a reference
and one thousand per cent forget about getting on The
Scheme. He'd make personally sure of that, goddammit.
You'll be catheterizing old ones in Ballinasloe, he said.
Call it urology if you want. You'll reek of piss, man, I can
promise you that. All day every day, no matter how much
you scrub yourself. Have I made myself clear, my friend?
Yes, yes, I said. For all the medical shit, we were to call the
medical reg and the medical SHO directly, no problem.

Especially with anything to do with the heart or any of that blood-sugar nonsense. Good man, he said, and then off he went, and off I went to the res to get changed and await the coming of the night like a prisoner who'd been found guilty and sentenced for an unspecified crime that hadn't even been committed yet. I tried to reassure myself that at least the medics tended to be a bit nicer than the surgeons, so calling them was going to be preferable. But it was also widely known that they had their hands full in casualty, waging their own particular war, manning the gates of the hospital as if it had been beset by the hordes of Barbaria. They would never be able to come up to the wards to help us, but at the very least they might be apologetic about it. No matter how you cut it, we were on our own at night. Stuart staring at me with his big eyes reminded me that he knew this just as much as I did.

– And she's right about the burns unit, I said. The nurses practically run it by themselves. All you'd have to do is wave the hand. Chart some fluids, maybe rewrite a few drug kardexes.

My voice sounded disingenuous even to my own ears. I had that flash of irritation at him again. Why was I the one who was reassuring him? Weren't we all in the same boat? I didn't feel any more prepared for this type of work than he did, and God knows I didn't want to be here any more than him. I looked back at the newspaper. We could hear Lynda at the door of the res, inputting the code to get back in. The lock was temperamental, and it took her a few goes before we could hear the door open and her footsteps on the corridor getting closer. Stuart had been about to say something, but he stopped when he heard her.

— Jesus Christ, Ed's haemorrhoids must be at him, Lynda said as she came into the kitchen.

She stood in front of us for a second.

— As soon as he saw me coming round the corner he started flapping his arms at me like a bloody penguin.

She put the bag on the table and told us how much money we owed her. As usual Stuart only had a fifty, and this time Lynda took it from him.

— Food's on Stuart tonight then, she said.

She announced that she was going to go into the television room because the kitchen area was bloody freezing. We got up and followed her next door. We found her standing at the entrance to the room, having switched on the light.

— His coat's still there, she said.

She went in and sat on the first armchair. Stuart and I paused at the doorway and looked at Arnie's coat hanging in the corner. I sat next to Lynda, and Stuart took one of the armchairs across the way. The light was bright and Arnie's coat in the corner dominated our vision. It didn't help that it was a shade of blue that had a luminous glow under the glare.

— You'd think they'd remove it, Lynda said. I'm sure his folks would want it.

As she spoke she reached back and turned off the light and it was a relief to sit in the semi-darkness. The coat was still visible but not as obvious, and the bright blue was merely dark. I tried to avoid looking at it, but the more I did so, the more prominent it seemed. None of us liked to be reminded of Arnie and what had happened to him. It would have been a simple thing to send his coat to his family or even throw it away. But none of us had taken the initiative, and more than likely it was going to stay there for ever.

Our pagers didn't even go off once as we ate. We were tense with the anticipation that they would. It was only a matter of time before Colles, in particular, got back to us, or Private 1. But they didn't, and we sat in an uneasy silence, broken only by the sound of our eating. We didn't talk, and each of us was lost in our own thoughts or, more accurately, our private zones of blankness. None of us made the effort to turn the television on and we stared at its empty screen as if a riveting film was being shown on it. Stuart let out a big yawn but then remembered where he was and rushed to cover his mouth. Lynda looked at him, shaking her head almost imperceptibly, then back at the blank TV screen. She had her legs tightly crossed. I could see a short athletic sock on her left foot, a couple of inches of bare ankle skin above it. Her chair was next to mine and if she sat back properly in it our arms would make contact. Stuart was sitting against the other wall. He was barely touching his food and stared at the TV screen. Whatever invisible movie was playing on it was for him one of infinite worry and angst, it told the story of the human race, how doomed it was. Time passed and it now qualified as a significant interval since our pagers had gone off. If you told me it had been an hour I would have believed you, but then again if you told me it had only been a few minutes I would have believed that too. Lynda took her pager out and pressed the button to make sure the battery hadn't run out. Satisfied, she replaced it at her waist and took up her plastic fork again. None of us was going to comment on how quiet things were. Even acknowledging it felt like a risk. If you accused us of being superstitious we would have denied it vehemently, but of course we were. It was our only instrument of control. In this regard we weren't much different to primitives in a mysterious world whose organizing principle was arbitrary or missing entirely. So we sat there, trying not to acknowledge the rising hope that this would be one of those quiet nights we had heard about. Others had experienced them, but never us, nights when the hospital seemed at rest, peaceful and at ease. Each of us thought about this but were afraid to hope for it, and we said nothing to each other in case the possibility was struck down. Instead we watched the invisible display on the TV screen, whatever it was showing to each of us, as we slowly, methodically, finished our Chinese.

Lynda's pager went off.

— Johns, she said, looking at the number, but she didn't get up to answer it.

A couple of minutes went by and my pager went off.

   – Let me guess, she said.

I looked down at the bright green numbers.

   – Yep, Johns, I said, and I moved to answer it.

   – Don't, she said, and I sat back in my seat.

A minute of silence passed and anticipation was in the air, the three of us looking at each other. Even Stuart was smiling.

   – Wait for it, Lynda said.

Sure enough, Stuart's pager now went off.

   – Johns, he said, looking down at the number that appeared on it.

   – Bingo, Lynda said, and the three of us laughed.

Stuart got up to call the ward back and Lynda didn't stop him. As he stood at the door talking, we could hear the nurse's voice through the phone. They wanted more fluids charted. Also Bed 4 had spiked and they needed blood cultures.

— Tell them we did him already, Lynda shouted over her shoulder to Stuart. It's pointless to culture him again, they should just give him some paracetamol, for God's sake.

But Stuart was too polite. OK, OK, he kept saying into the phone, his face earnest with concentration. He put the phone down and came back over to the table. Lynda was annoyed.

— They damn well knew we were heading for our break, she said.

Stuart took his seat. His manner was very grave.

— That woman died as well, he said, the one that was cheyne stoking.

Lynda stared at him.

— Well, what did you think was going to happen?

Stuart looked down at the floor.

— They want us to go and pronounce her, he said.

Lynda looked at me and gave the slightest shake of her head.

– There's no rush with that, she said.

And there was something about the way she said it that made me laugh.

Nobody said anything for a while, and we sat in silence that seemed to vibrate like a noise inside our heads – you could hear in it the faint residue of our pagers from the last time they went off, several minutes ago now, but still appreciable as a low-grade hum. We had finished our food and the plastic containers lay on our laps. There was a coffee table in the centre of the room and both Lynda and I had our feet on it. An ashtray contained several weeks of overflowing ash. I was sitting too close to Lynda to get a proper look at her facial expressions and imagine what she was seeing when she looked at the TV screen, but I was sure that whatever it was would be more straight-forward than what Stuart was seeing, perhaps an action flick that was always going to be resolved at the end. She sat almost in a trance, holding her plastic fork suspended in mid-air. We were tired, and our tiredness and cold-ness seemed to be working in harmony with each other. My back ached, as well as the small bones of my hands and feet. I would have given anything to go to bed and wake up when it was light, the sun streaming through the window, when the rest of the world had also woken up and we weren't the only people on the planet who were awake. Not that tomorrow was something to look forward to. I had another long day in store. My team would be in the operating theatre, which meant that I would have to hang around until seven or eight for the evening ward round. It might even be later if something went pear-shaped during one of their operations. There was, however, the long weekend to look forward to. Miraculously we weren't on call. I wanted to ask Lynda what she was planning to do, but I didn't know how to broach the subject. The running joke among the other interns was that me and Stuart were in love with her, but this wasn't true. It was hard to explain exactly what was in our minds, what the relationship was, but it was something different than that.

Lynda laughed to herself. For a second it seemed to me that she had read my mind. She looked from one to the other of us, smiling.

— Liz told me she met Hanratty the other night, she said. At an arrest.

Stuart and I looked at her and she continued.

— Liz said he was wandering past in his tracksuit, apparently on his way to pick up his delivery from Ed. He saw everyone rushing down the corridor and he followed them, then he took over and started running the arrest. Afterwards he was hanging around, chatting to them – they couldn't get away from him, apparently.

Lynda laughed, but all I could think about was how great that would be. We would have to carry the cardiac arrest bleep later in the year, during our medical rotation, and I was already dreading it. Arrests were pure chaos and nobody seemed to ever know what was happening during them. The thought of being the first one on the scene was terrifying. What a relief it would be if a consultant showed up and told you what to do, where to stand, put some order or shape on the whole thing, especially if it was a cardiologist like Hanratty was – I wouldn't have cared what he was like otherwise, how pathetic or gormless. And anyway, he wasn't the worst of them, especially if you compared him with any of the surgeons.

— Sad sap, Lynda said.

I'd actually run into Hanratty a week or so back, towards the end of the day. I wasn't on call, but it was late and I was waiting for my surgical team to return from theatre for the evening dry round. One of the patients had developed chest pain and the nurse made me do an ECG even though it was obvious there was nothing wrong with the man, it was probably just gas. I was on my way back after returning the machine to the ward where I'd borrowed it from. As I walked I held the ECG up in front of me and was squinting at it when Hanratty walked by.

— Here, he said. Give me a gander. Jesus, the look on your face. They're not that difficult, you know.

I was happy to stand there and let him look at it, although I was conscious of the time. I'd be in trouble with Sharif if the team returned from theatre and I wasn't at the nurses' station waiting to give them updates on the inpatients. We had about fifty in, and I would be expected to give a one-liner on each, the whole team looking at me, exhausted after being on their feet all day taking out people's stomachs and oesophaguses.

— Sinus, Hanratty said, holding the ECG up in the air. And what you have here is just early take-off, do you see that? Is that what you were worried about?

Were you thinking that was ST elevation? A common mistake. Mind you, these waves are a bit peaked – what's his potassium?

I said I didn't know, but he was staring hard at the piece of paper and not really listening. I hadn't thought it was ST elevation at all and was pretty confident the ECG was OK. Nevertheless, I acted the part of the attentive student. There was something pitiful about him. Everyone in the hospital knew that he'd had an affair with one of the American medical students. His wife, who was also one of the consultants, an endocrinologist, kicked him out and then the student dumped him and started going out with one of the Senior House Officers. Hanratty was apparently sleeping in the echo room down at Hospital 7, on the bench that during the day the patients lie up on to have their hearts evaluated, to assess whether their valves are leaking like sieves, or to visualize how old the muscle is biologically, how much life is left in it, how many more beats it has. Hanratty was wearing jeans and runners and a big jumper and looked to be on his way out for a walk. He reeked of depression, and I wanted to get away from him and get the ECG back from him and be on my way. At least now I would be able to tell Sharif that I had run things by cardiology, and that would quieten him down. Thankfully Hanratty's mobile rang, and he took it out of his pocket and answered it, handing the ECG back to me.

   – Better go, he said after finishing the call. My food's here. They're getting to know me there now. When I call them they say, *Same again, doctor?*

He put on a Chinese accent when he said the last part and then he slapped me on the shoulder and away he went. When I told Lynda all this she just shook her head.

   – She won't even let him near the kids. He's been on his knees to her begging, apparently. The echo nurses say there's the smell of him in the morning – they have to air the place out before letting any of the patients in, they have to open all the windows and tidy up his mess.

Stuart wasn't paying any attention. He was still fretting, staring at the television screen. Lynda nudged me and both of us looked over at him. He had barely touched his food.

   – Aren't you hungry, Stuart? Lynda asked.

He turned to us.

– They'll want to clear that bed, he said.

At first we didn't know what he was on about.

– Before they bring her down to the morgue,
he added.

– Well, Lynda said, they'd better make sure she's
dead first.

Again, the way she said it made me laugh.

– Casualty will need it as well, Stuart said, the bed,
that is.

– Yeah, well away off with you then, Lynda said back
at him. I'm finishing my dinner in peace.

Stuart looked at me but didn't move, and the three of
us continued to sit there in silence. It was absolutely
freezing. The res was a parody of a house, with its
sterile empty kitchen and its old fridge that only contained small cartons of milk, about fifty of them, and its
ancient microwave, and here, where we were sitting, a
shell of a living room. Certainly there was no fireplace,
just torn armchairs laid against the walls, the whole

thing a pre-fab that had been grudgingly added on to the end of the hospital. We hadn't even taken off our white coats.

Lynda sat back in her seat, her eyes closed, and now I was able to look at her properly. I expected any second for her eyes to open, but I didn't look away from the detail of her features and their sharpness. She'd done some modelling, apparently, and you could see that in her face, which seemed to be moving closer to me the harder I stared at it. And then her two eyes opened, as green as cat's eyes, looking back at me. The heat of embarrassment lit up my face and I looked to the floor, then shifted around pretending to be looking for something about my person. Lynda yawned and stretched out her arms. Then she sat forward, pulling her white coat tightly around her.

— It'll be quiet now, she said, so why don't I go first.

Stuart and I stared at her. She'd been talking about splitting up the night for weeks so it was hard to believe that she actually meant it for real this time. She stood up and handed me her pager, which I accepted casually, as if it was no big deal.

– Call me on my mobile at two a.m., she said. Then one of you two can sleep.

With that she was gone and Stuart and I sat in silence as if we were afraid to breathe. I held Lynda's pager in my hand, and perhaps I was only imagining that it felt warm from having been so recently attached to her waist. I gripped it tightly. Neither of us said anything and it seemed like it had been an age since she had left. Our silent pagers created their own tension which rose to an excruciating pitch. It would have been better if they had gone off, we could already hear their sound in our minds. Stuart had leaned forward in what looked like an uncomfortable position. Every muscle in his body was contracted, his jaw seemed to be clamped shut, and a ridge of muscle ran down the side of his cheek as he continued to stare into the depths of the blank television screen. It didn't take much to imagine him throwing up, a silent heaving of the chest and the sudden need to dive over to the waste bin in the corner. For Stuart, the hospital must have resembled one of those medieval paintings of hell, swarming with devils and the wretched. The closer you looked at it, the more you picked up on some new detail of cruelty within the image that would be teeming with such incidents. You might stand in front of the painting a hundred times and find something

35

new in it each time, somebody's isolated experience of misery that you hadn't noticed until then. Our role in the painting, mine and his and Lynda's, was of course open to question. Most of the time it felt like we were at one with the miserable and the damned, stripped to our scalded skin, just like the patients in the grand scheme of things, equally without power or agency; but sometimes we were ranked with the junior ghouls or devils you could see directing the show, whip in hand, shepherding the poor naked souls towards the flames.

I pulled one of the newspapers over from the pile on the chair near me and tried to focus on it. The headlines made no sense, which was always the case during the night. The day's world seemed abstract, the zone the newspaper referred to far away, its concerns having nothing to do with us here. On the front page was a photograph of a politician pointing at something over her head bearing the slogan Forward Together. It made no sense to me. In all this time nobody bleeped us and I started to think that things might not be so bad after all. But then Stuart's pager went off and the sound was a piercing reminder that the hospital was still out there. At first Stuart didn't move an inch, but then he jumped to his feet and practically sprinted over to the phone, as if this was the moment of his reckoning.

It wasn't a number either of us was familiar with, and Stuart dialled it, then stood at the phone for ages waiting for a nurse to pick up. This sort of thing would drive Lynda crazy, when the nurses paged us but then wandered off to do something and weren't there to answer the phone when we called back. She'd either hang up on them or yell at them when they finally appeared on the other end. But there was none of that from Stuart, who dutifully waited for someone to pick up, which they eventually did. Hospital 5, he mouthed to me, his hand over the receiver. I reminded him that we were the surgical interns and Hospital 5 was covered by the medical intern, but he was pre-empted by the nurse on the other end, whose voice I could also hear. The patient had an abscess drained the day before, she said, so technically we were covering. If we had a problem with that we were to take it up with the medical intern. I would have argued the point a little, Lynda definitely would have, but Stuart told the nurse OK, OK, we'd be right over. He put the phone down and looked at me, but God knows what he expected me to say. I stood up and the two of us headed down the corridor, not the one which led back to the main hospital, but the other corridor which led outdoors and into the night. We passed a row of empty rooms and came to the end of the res. When we opened the door the wind caught it and slammed it against the external wall. The breeze hit us in our faces. It was laced with moisture. We emerged into the small consultant car park, which was empty. The wind caught the door again and slammed it shut behind us. Stuart and I stood still in the fresh air, feeling the noisy whip of it. We hadn't been outdoors since coming to work the previous morning, which seemed like an eternity ago. The rain was pure delight, and we both laughed for some reason. Down to our left you could see the entire body of the main hospital, a vast industrial structure, not particularly lit up, its hull dotted by an intense beading of security lights which didn't seem to have much of a range to them. We went through the small car park to get to the entrance to Hospital 5, which was not part of the main campus but a separate and much older building. It was the original site of the hospital, emerging from some voluntary enterprise started by the nuns, but to be honest I hadn't much clue about the history of the place, it wasn't written down or exhibited and it didn't seem to be of interest or a source of pride to anyone. Hospital 5 contained the infectious diseases unit in addition to a long-stay section which was a home for old people who'd been institutionalized for decades, and possibly forgotten about entirely. The geriatric intern covered them, and it was an easy number by all accounts, apparently they were able to sleep the whole night through, and even had time to shower and have breakfast the next morning before starting their day's work. I hadn't been in this part of the hospital since I was a medical student. It was the best place to go then because of how sick the patients were. Half of them were at death's door and displayed the full range of physical signs that we had to pick up on for our finals; their chests and abdominal cavities were full of effusions, their leaking hearts displaying the textbook murmurs, their livers and spleens so swollen within their cachectic frames that even we students could see them, you could practically spot them pushing out through their pyjamas from the end of the bed.

Stuart and I stood outside the main entrance. Our giddiness at the fresh breeze eased and it now simply felt cold and we wanted to go inside. On the other side of the building the new car park stretched off in the direction of the floodlit council flats. There were plans for a cancer institute, but so far it was nothing more than a dirt surface that was also half a building site, a recent extension project that had commenced but then seemingly stalled. We pressed the intercom but it took a while for anyone to answer. Finally there was a buzz and the main door clicked and we pushed it open. When we passed through the entrance our ghostly images showed on the monitor in the corner of the ceiling. We went through another door and down the stately hallway, before climbing the broad staircase, its steps made of smooth stone, old convent marble, the portraits of long-dead doctors lining the wall. Our footsteps, every sound we made, seemed to echo.

When we got to the nurses' station on the third floor it was empty, but we saw them down the far end at the meds trolley, doing their rounds, a student nurse and an older one in an agency uniform. They didn't know why we were there, and we thought for a second the whole thing must have been a mistake. But then another nurse appeared out of nowhere and told us to follow her, and she led us halfway down the corridor to a side passageway that we had walked by without noticing. She stopped in front of a single room.

– Don't take any shit from him, the nurse said as she knocked on the door.

She was already pushing it open when she stopped and turned to us again.

– And Christ, she said, make sure you double glove – this one's viral load is through the roof. Totally non-compliant.

I asked her where their supply room was.

— I've got it all set up for you here, she said.

On the ledge by the door were blood culture bottles, and a tin foil tray containing gauze and syringes. I could see there was even a tourniquet. The nurse pushed the door in and we saw that there were two beds in the room. Two prison officers sat guarding one of them, and in that bed I could make out a gaunt face looking out at me from under the blankets, the pupils capturing some of the illumination that came through from a light just outside the window. The nurse brought us over to the other bed which at first glance I had thought was empty.

— Now Thomas, the nurse said to its invisible occupant, these doctors are here to take blood from you, so rise up my boy.

As she spoke she went round to the other side of the bed, and there was some movement in the bedclothes and the sound of a voice which moaned and complained.

— Are you refusing, Thomas, are you? the nurse said. That's fine, no problem at all. We'll just document that in the notes, Thomas. Now get up and put your legs over this side.

As she spoke she was already lifting his legs and swivelling them round so that the rest of his body had no choice but to follow. He was a skeletal and sickly looking figure. We stood and waited for him to stir. He was shivering, muttering to himself, complaining. It was hard to make out what he was saying, but there were curse words and he called her a fucking bitch.

— Are you refusing, Thomas? No problem. I'll let the team know in the morning. We'll just have to discharge you, if that's what you want. You can get your methadone somewhere else. It's all the same to me, Thomas.

As this was going on we became aware of an awful stench, the smell of moist infected flesh. Below the waist the man was practically naked, his pyjamas loose, open and stained. A thick dressing pad clung to his lower leg, but it didn't seem to be attached very firmly. Stuart just stood there, and it was clear he was leaving things up to me, but I waited too and stood my ground, prompting him to take a step towards the man. After all, it was he whom they had called in the first place.

   – I'm not lettin' him near me, the man said. I had you before so I did.

   – Thomas, that's enough now, the nurse said.

   – He's bleedin' dangerous so he is. He put the fuckin' needle straight into me bone.

Stuart stood in front of the man, his shoulders slumped. He didn't move. I took the tin foil tray off him and got my tourniquet out of my pocket. The man was grinning at me. He was fully awake now, even enjoying himself.

   – And here's Tweedle-fuckin-dee, he said.

There was laughter, and when I looked over I saw that it had come from the prison officers. The head of the man they were guarding was poking out from beneath the sheets, his eyes wide open looking at me, dots of light in the centre of the pupils, a hairless head.

I walked towards the patient sitting on the edge of the bed. He was watching me closely. The smell of his abscess came in pulses – it was the worst I had ever experienced and caused an instant nausea to rise, which then vanished just as quickly. I tried not to breathe in as I put the tourniquet on his tense arm. He sat on his hands and made no effort to help. I knew straight away that he had no veins. You can tell on the first touch with some arms, there's a certain sheen, a hardness and a coldness to them. I knew already that the exercise was futile. On the man's knuckles were homemade tattoos and on his thin arms various marks and scars, and evidence of a previous burn. I asked him to clench his fist, but he didn't do anything. The nurse had disappeared. I took up his arm and looked around it, but it was as if it was entirely bloodless, containing no vasculature of any description. It was a damp limb of cold, hard flesh. He started complaining again but I ignored him and stuck the needle in at the elbow, more or less randomly. He didn't flinch, but when I moved the needle again he let out a loud shout.

— You hit the bleedin' nerve, he said, and pulled his arm away, causing the syringe to fall on the floor.

Stuart's pager went off and he hurried off to answer it.

— Sorry, I said.

— Here, give it to me will ya, the man said, but I

ignored him, slapping his arm with the back of my hand to try and bring up a vein.

— You're not tryin' again, he said. I mean it. I don't give a fuck what Big Bessie out there says.

There was more laughter, and I looked around to see again that it had come from the prison officers. They weren't looking over at me but they were following every word, getting great entertainment out of it all. Their man's head was still poking out from the blankets, the little discs of light staring at me. I took the tourniquet off and put it on the other arm.

— You'll never fuckin' get one, the patient said.

I thought I felt a vein, but after some time realized it was just the elbow tendon.

— I'm tellin' ya, the man said, here, give it to me, I'll get it for you.

I stopped and he knew I was considering his offer. He motioned to me to pull the curtain around so that the guards wouldn't see.

— Come on the fuck, he said.

The guards were leaning back against the wall. I guessed that they had their eyes closed. I put a clean needle on the syringe and handed it to the man. He snatched it off me, giving a little laugh to himself. He pushed himself further over the edge of the bed, pulled his pyjama bottoms down a bit and leaned backwards. In the meantime, Stuart came back in and stood behind me, trying to make sense of the scene in front of him, the patient lying back holding the syringe in one hand, while with the other he pressed down on his groin looking for a vein. He moved his hand around a bit and then brought the syringe down, and there was a small give and you could see the chamber fill up with dark fluid. He slowly drew out the plunger and another rush of blood came out and Stuart and I stood looking at it. That's plenty, I told the patient, but he filled it a bit more before pulling out the syringe and holding it, drops of blood dripping from the needle tip on to his pyjamas.

He was grinning, and held up the syringe so that I had to reach over to take it. He let me have it with a slight resistance. The syringe was warm from the blood.

— Put it into the bottles before it clots, he said. That's fuckin' gold that is. Liquid gold I'm tellin' ya.

— Here's a bit of gauze, I said, and handed it to him, but he let it drop to the floor.

He lay back on the bed delighted with himself, a widening red stain appearing on his pyjama bottoms.

— Tell Big Bessie I fuckin' helped yiz OK?

I told him that I would, and Stuart and I left the room.

As we walked down the corridor I could sense Stuart's brooding presence a couple of steps behind me. It took a minute to locate the supply unit next to the sluice room and I had to shout down to the nurse to ask her what the code was. She only whispered it back to me, but the sound reverberated along the corridor. Once we were inside I transferred the blood from the syringe into the culture bottles, putting alcohol wipes on the tops of the bottles and passing the needles through them to keep the sample sterile, a trick Lynda had shown me. I was about to throw out the rest of the blood, but changed my mind and instead grabbed an FBC tube and a U&E tube and filled them also just in case they were needed.

It seemed a waste to discard the blood that had been so hard to obtain. Stuart stood to the side the whole time, uselessly, not helping in any way, not saying a word. Something was up with him, but I left him stewing for another couple of minutes.

– What's wrong with you? I eventually said to him.

– Jesus, you took a bit of a risk there, he said with a nervous chuckle.

I was irritated and had to stop myself from lashing out. For a few minutes the only sound came from my movements as I worked on the samples, taking care as I discarded the syringe into the sharps box, the needle still dripping dark blood from its tip. Each drop of blood would contain millions of virus particles. I wondered if their presence altered the colour of the blood in any way, darkening it perhaps. I moved very slowly, deliberately, the whole time nursing my own indignation at Stuart. If it hadn't been for me, we would have still been trying to get the blood from that guy. I took out a pen and wrote on the labels of the glass bottles, something that was always difficult to do legibly. It would be so much better if we were allowed to put stickers on them, but micro were opposed to this for some reason. I finished with the bottles and threw the plastic in the biohazard bin as there were some blood stains on it. I had to ask Stuart to move. He was standing there, watching me. He looked so pathetic that I felt sorry for him again, and whatever annoyance I felt towards him was ebbing away. I finished with all the bottles and labels. I double-bagged the samples, and to ease the tension between us I asked him who it was that had bleeped him.

– There's someone on Patrick Duns they want reviewed, he said.

– What's wrong with them?

– Breathing issues apparently.

We left the supply room and I placed the plastic bags in the out tray at the nurses' station. There was no sign of any of the nurses. We walked down the corridor, then descended the broad staircase and slipped out the front door of Hospital 5. Again the breeze in the consultant car park came as a surprise. We stood in it for a minute before getting cold and heading back into the res, which was the quickest way to access the main part of the hospital. It took us a few goes to get the door code to work, and then Stuart held the door open to make sure the wind didn't catch it. We went past the kitchen and along the other corridor that would lead us back to the main hospital. One of the bedroom doors was closed, and I guessed this must be Lynda's room. I slowed down as we went past it, allowing Stuart to go on a few paces, and I paused briefly to listen at her door. There was no sound, but then again I couldn't imagine Lynda being a loud sleeper. I would have guessed that she slept only superficially, just millimetres below the surface of consciousness, and only then for a few hours, dreamless, and that she had no trouble turning her thoughts off at will, like a tap, before emerging a couple of hours later completely refreshed, springing out of bed when her alarm sounded. I moved on before Stuart turned around, and then we were in the dark connecting corridor, in the tunnel that reminded me of a space station, and it was even colder now, making it even easier to imagine that we were adrift from the earth, in one of her system's remote or outer zones. The door at the other end was partially open and we pushed through it. We were back in the main hospital, and the air changed again, becoming warmer, though you could never describe the hospital as being warm exactly. Without needing to discuss it, we automatically went up the stairwell to avoid Private 1 and then headed quickly through Private 2. When we got to Patrick Duns the nurses were annoyed that we had taken so long.

– He's down there, one of them said. His light's on.

We walked in the direction they had indicated to the bottom ward, which was a six-bed. The curtains had been pulled around the bed nearest the door and the light was on overhead, illuminating the patient's cubicle. The other five beds in the ward were in darkness and sounds of snoring could be heard coming from them. I pulled back the curtain to see a bald barrel-chested man sitting on the bed with his pyjama top open. He barely registered us and was leaning over, concentrating on his breathing, his hands gripping his shins. He had an oxygen mask on and you could tell immediately that he was in a bad way. Stuart and I stood looking at him. A nurse appeared beside us.

– He's been like this since the start of my shift, she said. He seems to be getting worse.

– Did you call the reg? Stuart said to her, in an obvious panic.

– That's your job, she said, and walked away.

Stuart stared after her, then looked at me. I knew that he wanted nothing to do with this and in his head had already delegated everything to me. He would do anything I asked of him but not otherwise contribute. I was basically on my own. I went over to the man and introduced myself, but he didn't look up. I shot some questions at him but he was in no position to respond, he was so focused on his breathing, and I knew it was pointless to try to get any sort of a history out of him. I put a few half-hearted questions to him all the same. Do you have any chest pain? Palpitations or dizziness? What about a headache? Has this sort of thing ever happened before? Did it come on suddenly or gradually? Any family history of anything? But it was pointless – the man ignored me as if he didn't hear me, he was in his own world. I went back to the bottom of the bed, to where Stuart was standing.

— We'd better do everything, I said to him. Do you want to go off and get the ECG machine?

Stuart's relief was plain, which irritated me. Sending him to get the ECG machine was one of Lynda's tricks. He'd be gone for ages looking for it, which would give me some time to get my thoughts organized so that I could write a proper note in the chart, which in many ways was the most important thing. The note was how you would be judged the next day when the patient's team arrived. They would go through it to see what tests you had ordered, what treatment you had started, what your differential diagnosis was. Someone this sick would require at least a page. It was a way of putting your side of the story first, your version of events, making clear the ambiguity of the situation, no matter how clear and obvious it appeared to them in the light of day, that it could have been literally anything that you were dealing with, a heart attack, a stroke, some sort of aneurysm or rupture, and look at everything you did to investigate the situation, for God's sake, you did everything you could think of, therefore how could you possibly be to blame?

— I'll check Colles ward, Stuart said, but I might have to go over to the geri's ward. The one there works better.

He ran off. I turned to the man again. From the barrel chest on him it was obvious he had emphysema. There were inhalers on the side locker next to the bed, as well as a cigarette lighter. I took out the stethoscope and put it on his back. His pyjamas and the vest underneath were ringing wet. Small pockets of water had collected in the hollow indents above his shoulder blades. I placed the stethoscope at different areas on his back, but I couldn't hear anything over the noise that was coming from the oxygen mask. A different nurse was standing at the bottom of the bed now.

— What do you think? she asked me.

— Could be anything, I said.

I reached over and pressed on the man's abdomen. It was distended but soft and I was fairly sure that he was simply fat. He didn't flinch or groan when I pushed deeply into it. This was more of a chest thing than an abdominal thing. I turned again to the nurse.

— I'd better do a blood gas, I said, looking at her.

— Don't ask me, the nurse said, if you have to do it, do it.

— Yeah, I think I have to do one.

— And by the way, I called the medical reg for you, the nurse said. She said they're stuck in casualty but if you want you can call her after you've assessed the patient and she'll talk to you over the phone.

— She'll want to know the pO_2, I said. I'd definitely better do a blood gas then. Thanks.

— Well there's your answer then, the nurse said. The code for the stock room is four fours.

I left the patient and went down the corridor to the stock room. I had to input the code a few times before I was able to open the door, and found myself standing in the middle of the room, looking up at its packed shelves that almost reached the ceiling. These rooms were a source of constant annoyance to us. Each ward had their own one, but they were all arranged differently from each other and there was no standardized system within the hospital, no organizing principle, or at least not one that any of us could figure out. As a result, we would spend half the night in these rooms looking for things, staring uselessly up at the shelving units that reared above us and were packed with the supportive material most bodies will need at some point in their existence. The sheer volume of the equipment was extraordinary – it was hard to credit the number of ways in which it was possible or even necessary to intervene in the repair and maintenance of the human body, to pierce it or dress it or patch it up, to supplement it with nutrition or fluids or alternatively drain it in a variety of ways, its effusions, collections, exudates. If you were to buy the human body in a toy shop, all of this equipment would come with it in the box, or perhaps you would pay extra for it, like you do with the action figures children play with. It was a reminder of how vulnerable to injury the body is, how much it is in need of continual attention, the endless number of ways in which it can burn or leak or ooze or swell or become internally stuck, dependent as it is on an array of naturally occurring inner drains and ducts which are easily blocked or clogged with debris or cellular matter, and prone to narrowing by tumours, strictures, scar tissue. Just for the skin there was a bewildering array of dressings that I always found hard to distinguish from each other, each serving a special purpose, transparent or covered ones, adhesives of different sizes, mostly plastic, plasters or gauze and mesh for internal wounds or damage to the fascia, a whole container of cotton wool, another that was full to the brim with rolls and rolls of tape, IV cannulae of different gauges that looked like toothbrushes in their little boxes, their green or blue or orange needles. And then on the bottom shelves was all the hardware, the various drains that were particularly necessary on the surgical wards, nasogastric tubes, urinary catheters, chest drains, as well as the procedure kits, aseptically wrapped and sealed, like miniature implements of torture, bone marrow trephines, lumbar punctures, with their hollow bores and guidewire needles that looked far worse and could do more damage than the needle itself, or those kits for draining the cavities, both pleural and abdominal. It must have taken five whole minutes for me to finally locate the blood gas packets in a drawer, the very last place I checked, of course, as if they had been hidden away on purpose. I grabbed a tinfoil tray and some cotton wool and a handful of alcohol wipes and headed back to the patient.

He was in a very bad way, possibly getting worse. You wouldn't have needed any medical training to know this, he was barely alert now, his breathing tired, the sweat still pouring out of him. He was groaning out of pain or exhaustion. I knelt down beside the bed and took his arm, turning it over palm-up to find the radial pulse at his wrist. His arm was floppy and I took one of his pillows and rested it on my knee with his arm on top of it. I hated doing blood gases. There was a knack to them that you either had or didn't have. You had to feel for the pulse with the thick pad of your index finger while at the same time trying to coordinate the location of the artery with the tip of the needle that you held in your other hand, ready to spear it into the underside of the wrist. Sometimes it was hard to detect the pulse at all, or even if it was plainly there according to your finger, the needle would go in and out but come back empty. It didn't take much for you to feel the scraping of the bone, and the patient would also feel that, exquisitely, and they'd let you know about it. And then if you were rooting around too long you'd cause the useless bleeding of venous rather than arterial blood and dark liquid would ebb slowly into the syringe and you would have to start the process all over again with the patient staring down at you with gritted teeth and tears in their eyes and hoping or even praying with all their might that you would get it this time. But, bingo! I couldn't believe my luck when a small jet of bright red liquid shot into the syringe immediately and I gently tugged on the plunger to fill the chamber with far more blood than was necessary. I looked up at the patient, half-expecting him to congratulate me for getting it first time, but he was still in his own world, his arm was limp and I doubt he was even aware of what I was doing. I removed the needle from the underside of his wrist and stuck the tip of it into the small rubber cube that came in the packet, and then pressed some cotton wool tightly against his inner wrist. I let it go after half a minute though, which wasn't long enough to avoid a haematoma, but I couldn't hang around too long. I hurried away holding the aluminium container with the syringe in it and left the ward.

The blood gas machine was situated outside ICU on the third floor. I practically sprinted there. It was the first thing the reg would want to know when I called her – the pO_2, the pCO_2, the sats. I'd learned the hard way on previous occasions when I had had to call her. She wouldn't be interested in anything subjective. My opinion about how the guy looked didn't count, the fact that I thought he seemed to be really sick, or that I was worried about him. Subjective terms like that would make her bristle, especially if my voice was infused with panic. She wanted the facts, discrete pieces of information, and if I didn't have them she would feel no onus to do anything other than tell me to go and get those pieces of information and then call her back. Getting people to help you in this job had the contours of a game, a contest between you and them, and you had to make sure that the obligation was always on the other side, you couldn't give them an easy out by not having the correct information, which would for them add up to a form of deniability, leaving you on your own, just you and your sick patient.

Going up the ICU stairwell, it was hard not to think about Arnie. The stairwell had been closed until recently. When they reopened it, it was a surprise to find it was just the same as before, though I'm not sure what improvements could have been made. Some netting perhaps. A higher banister or some protective glass. Perhaps a phone number that people could call if they were in a bad way; or some sort of display that they have at certain cliffs or popular bridges, flowers or lights which come on in the darkness, a message that you are not alone, that sort of thing. But there was none of that, and the corridor was the way it had always been. In any case, people didn't go this way since it reopened, they tended to use the stairwell at the other end of the corridor. But I made a point of coming this way, and I never met anyone else in it and it was always in darkness. When I got to the top floor I couldn't resist looking over and wondering for the hundredth time how on earth anyone could survive the jump, which Arnie did for a couple of weeks. There must have been something to cushion his fall, perhaps a laundry skip. Or maybe he changed his mind at the last instant and was able to grab on to the railing or even propel himself over towards the second-floor landing. The more I stared down, the more of a mystery it was. The odds against surviving it would have been one in a million, and even then he would have been left with a drastic paralysis, maybe even ventilated for ever. But I don't believe he had any of that, and they say that he died of the head injury but was otherwise more or less intact. He never regained consciousness, which must have made things worse for his family. You would see them in the corridor outside ICU if the staff were working on him or they simply needed a break, his elderly parents and an older sister who was the image of him.

I jogged down the long corridor which sat directly above the link corridor but was typically empty, even during the day. I passed the operating theatres and, next to them, the sterilization area where all of the soiled linen of the hospital was sent. I could hear the noise from the industrial cleaners hard at work, getting the place ready for the next day. A group of porters were playing some sort of game with the plastic crates, throwing them along the wet tiled floor which in places had large puddles of water. They looked at me when I went past before deciding I was nobody to worry about, the night sister in other words, who was known to patrol the hospital looking for just this type of carry-on. The porters continued with their game.

My swipe card never worked in ICU, so I had to ring the doorbell, and it took an eternity before someone at the nurses' station eventually buzzed me in. A group of people had gathered in the relatives' room directly across from the small room where the blood gas machine was located. The people in the relatives' room were cramped into the tiny space, huddled around each other and entirely silent. A child slept on the couch with blankets thrown over her. I set down the tin foil tray on the worktop and separated the ABG needle from the syringe and put it in the sharps container. I squeezed some of the blood into the portal of the machine and pressed the button to analyze the sample. A message appeared saying there was no paper in the machine. I stared at it in a rage for what felt like a long time. I started checking the cupboards underneath, but they were all locked. The only one I could open had an array of coffee mugs in it with people's names written on them. I left the room and went into the ICU. It was fairly quiet and peaceful, the only sounds coming from the regular beeping of the machines by each of the beds and the hush of the ventilators from the twenty-odd berths, each of the patients intubated and unconscious. A couple of nurses were at the raised central area which was an island in the middle of the room, an embankment full of monitors. They were having a conversation and I didn't want to interrupt them, but the longer I stood there the more agitated I became, especially as it was just a social conversation they were having. Eventually one of them turned to me and said, Paper, right? She took a deep breath and told me to follow her, leading me back to where the blood gas machine was. She removed a key from around her neck and opened one of the cupboards and took out a roll of paper. After she handed it to me she must have spotted my confusion because she took it off me again and inserted it into the machine.

– Why don't they teach you stuff like this? she said.

A little strip of paper came out with the results of the reading. I was delighted. The results were consistent with arterial blood, and the pO_2 wasn't actually too bad. Perhaps the reg wouldn't come up to review the patient now given that the numbers were OK. I threw the syringe into the sharps box and hurried back down the corridor in the direction of the ward. When I got back and passed the nurses' station I showed them the small piece of paper, practically waving it above my head in triumph. Stuart's ECG machine was in the corridor outside the six-bed room where the patient was. I went in and opened the curtain. Lynda was standing at the head of the patient's bed. She had her hand on the man's chest and there was what looked like an IV cannula sticking out of his chest wall just below the clavicle. A whistle of air was coming out of it and Lynda held it firmly in position against the patient's chest wall, which was now moving up and down nicely, deeper and not as fast as it had been earlier. His eyes were open and he was lying back staring at the ceiling in what looked like a state of pure relief. The whistling noise from the cannula was occurring in tandem with every breath that the man took. It was a few moments before the picture made sense to me. Now I recognized what Lynda had done, how she had placed the cannula in the exact position recommended by the textbooks in the event of an emergency such as this, the second intercostal space in the mid-clavicular line. I could have even stood there and recited the list of clinical signs that we had had to learn in list form for Finals – the hypertympanic chest, the midline tracheal shift, the low or even absent breath sounds – all of which were classic for a tension pneumothorax. Lynda didn't say a word, but it was easy to detect her satisfaction. There would have been a loud hiss when she put the needle into his chest, like a football bursting. The man's relief would have been instant, and she was still buzzing from it. In the short, intense time I had known her I had never seen her like this – her face was beaming out at us. She couldn't stop smiling, and even broke into little runs of spontaneous laughter. I noticed Stuart standing there as well, behind me, blending into the curtain. He was looking at the floor but raised his head when I turned to him.

– I called her, he said, guessing my thoughts.

I started to say something but stopped. Lynda was watching us with amusement, still bent over holding the cannula that she had plunged into the man's chest.

— Here, she said to me, give Stuart your pager. You look wrecked.

— It's not two a.m. yet, I said.

— The reg is coming up to put in a chest drain. She said she'd let me do it. You might as well go.

I stood for a moment, then handed my pager to Stuart and headed off the ward, past the nurses' station. The nurses were sitting behind the desk and they both looked up at me as I went by. I walked off the ward and out past the entrance to Johns, stopping at the large window of the short link corridor which led to the private wing. I had to make an effort to see out through my own reflection glowering back at me in the dark glass. The scattered lights of the hospital, the council flats and the local industrial estate barely penetrated the thick night. There was no sign of the city beyond, and faith alone was needed to tell you it was still there. Now it was just my own reflection staring back at me and the world outside vanished. In my pocket I came across the piece of paper with the blood gas results, but I didn't bother returning to put them in the notes. They were irrelevant now.

As I was about to head off, one of the nurses came out of Johns ward looking for me.

— So this is where you're hiding, she said. We've been waiting an age for you lot.

I wanted to explain that she should call the others, but couldn't get the words out.

— Come on, she said. We need to clean out that room, get her ready.

I followed her on to the ward. She was carrying an IV bag and she went into the treatment room. I stood and waited for her. When she came out she seemed surprised to see me still standing there.

— It's that room over there, she said, in case you've forgotten.

She sensed my confusion and made a frustrated sound.

— Come on then, she said, and I followed her over to one of the side rooms.

I went into the room and the woman who had died earlier in the night was on the bed. Her family had gone and the woman was lying flat with only one pillow under her head rather than propped up as she had been before. A thick candle was lit on the bedside locker. The woman's eyes and mouth were wide open. She didn't seem as peaceful as she had done earlier, as if she had experienced some last-minute fright.

— Don't worry about the eyes, the nurse said. Noreen has a knack for getting them closed.

I stood at the bottom of the bed.

— Well, go on then, said the nurse.

I'd never pronounced anyone before and wasn't sure whether there was a proper way to do it, some protocol that I should be following. I picked up her arm and checked her pulse for a long time, but it was unclear if I was feeling one or if it was just my own. I rested the arm down then took out my stethoscope and moved to the lungs and the heart. I kept hearing sounds and it was hard to distinguish them from my own movements. But there were also other noises, groaning sounds that seemed to come from deep within the woman's body. I had heard it said that even after someone dies the body continues to produce sounds for minutes or even hours afterwards, as the gas and air escape. I had heard stories, perhaps they were urban myths, of interns who had pronounced people dead when they were in fact still alive and had to be returned from the morgue. I stood looking at the woman for a while. There wasn't any doubt that she was dead despite what I was hearing or imagining that I was hearing. I took out my pen torch and shone it into her open eyes and her pupils registered no change. They were dilated and unresponsive, entirely black to the light, and this settled things. I turned and looked at the nurse.

– She's dead, I said.

– No shit Sherlock. Now go and document it, will you? Come on, A & E have been calling every two minutes looking for the bed. The night sister's been on to us as well.

I left the room and went over to the chart trolley and took out the dead woman's notes. They were so thick and disorganized it took a while to find a blank page. I wrote a long note, detailing my examination, taking more time than was necessary, writing too much, words that in all likelihood would never be read. Then I stood up and walked off the ward and to the res, going the back way to avoid the private wards. The rest of the night must have been unremarkable because I don't remember any of it. I have a memory of waking on the hard sheets of the res bed, the air chilly, the morning sun to the point of blindness streaming through the windows, and feeling the blessed relief of being back in the world again, having returned to it intact like a rebirth. But I have no way of knowing if that was truly that next morning or another morning altogether, or even whether it happened like that at all but was instead some manufactured memory.

I didn't see Lynda for the rest of the week, except from a distance, and then it was the long weekend. Everyone knew about what had happened, and more than once I heard the other interns talking in the res about what she had done and presumably what I had or had not done. They lowered their voices or stopped talking altogether when I came into the room. Even the SHOs and registrars knew about the whole thing, and Sharif, my registrar, said that this would get her on to The Scheme for sure. She was invited to do the clinical case presentation on the Wednesday at surgical grand rounds, where her quick actions were interpreted by the Chair of Surgery as evidence of the great clinical training they were providing for us. (The Chair of Medicine had made the same claim earlier in the week.) Her case presentation was titled Emergent Management of Tension Pneumothorax. My consultant, Professor Lynch, was chairing the meeting, and as Lynda went up to the lectern, he stood leering at her. She ignored him and spent an awkward minute orientating the overhead projector. She had made an effort for the occasion and was dressed elegantly. Afterwards Lynch threw a lot of questions at her, clearly trying to catch her out, but she was able to deal with them all without any problem.

Later that day I passed Stuart on the corridor but we barely acknowledged each other, as though we were merely familiar to one another but not otherwise acquainted. Then the moment passed and he carried on with his team and I with mine. We were both on our consultant rounds, going between the wards where the majority of our patients resided – Johns for him, Bennetts for me – and were on our way to some of the outlier wards. Sharif, my registrar, was at his most obsequious with Professor Lynch, asking about the consultant's kids, they were in university, right, Trinity? And did the professor have any plans for the long weekend, going anywhere nice with Mrs Lynch? Oh, that's right, the rugby's on, so who was going to win the big match then? The older man was gruff and minimal in his replies. Professor Lynch was pre-retirement but was still sharp and unpleasant and could turn on you quickly. In general, the surgical teams were more hierarchical and less collaborative than the medical specialities, even quite militaristic. Rank was everything, and being the intern placed you at the bottom of the ladder. Lynch never spoke to me on the ward rounds and was only vaguely aware of my presence, certainly he wouldn't have known my name. He only interacted with Sharif, but even with him he mainly communicated non-verbally, glaring at him or twitching with impatience to get him to move on to the next patient, indicating that he had heard enough about the person lying in the bed in front of him, whoever they were, whatever the hell was wrong with them. Once or twice on rounds Lynch could be counted upon to erupt at Sharif if his question wasn't answered to his satisfaction or if he felt that Sharif had glossed over, or was trying to hide, something. Lynch had a good nose for that sort of thing, from years of junior staff putting a spin on things or even lying outright to him. His outbursts were always sudden and fierce. And in those moments the look on Sharif's face was unforgettable.

Some colour would come into it, his speech would falter and he would try to hide his distress at this abrupt reminder of where he stood in the scheme of things and how he wasn't to forget it. Sharif would be quiet for a while, even a little sullen, but in fairness he would soon rebound, the guy was nothing if not resilient, and before the ward round ended he might even get in a few more questions about the consultant's plans for the weekend or his college-going kids. The only other people on the ward round were the ward sister and both SHOs, two gawky individuals who looked like brother and sister – it was only later that I found out they were going out with each other. The SHOs were on the next rung up from me on the hierarchy. They never said anything, their responsibility was to attend theatre and learn the basics of the surgical trade, suturing mainly, as well as executing some of the minor procedures, appendectomies, hernia repairs, varicose veins, in addition to assisting for the major cases, where, if they were lucky, they might get to make the first cut into the pristine skin, before spending the next four or five or six hours holding clamps in position until their hands cramped, providing intermittent suction on demand, perhaps being permitted to ligate the odd vessel, prior to carrying out the tedious business of closing up once Professor Lynch and Mr Sharif had completed the central task of the operation. Both of the SHOs were on the surgical training scheme, or The Scheme, as it was breathlessly referred to, and they were of no help to me in my daily work, quickly disappearing as soon as the ward round was over.

The rounds generally only took about thirty or forty minutes despite the large number of inpatients. Lynch would stand at the bottom of the patients' beds while Sharif whispered to him the briefest of summaries. Day 6 post-gastrectomy. No bowel sounds. NG tube still draining. Urinary catheter in situ, but beginning to mobilize, doing quite well overall. The ward sister would pipe up now and again, doing her best to contradict Sharif at every opportunity. He's Day 7 today actually, Mr Sharif. One of the girls thought she heard bowel sounds. He's really slow to mobilize in fact, should we be thinking of a nursing home? You would expect Sharif to grit his teeth, but he was deferential towards her too, Thank you sister, thank you sister, he would say, flashing a fake smile at her, while Lynch stared at him with outright hostility. He was a charmless and gruff old man, Lynch, with stubby fingers, and by all accounts he was a clumsy surgeon, certainly in comparison with Sharif who, in fairness to him, was, according to the SHOs and other registrars, a genuine whizz in the operating room. It was really Sharif who ran things, lingering after the round was over to run through the list of jobs, telling me to do this and this first, and I'd better do this and also this, and to absolutely one hundred per cent make sure that I went down to radiology and got this and this arranged asap, and to especially not forget about this, particularly this, otherwise Lynch would lose the rag altogether and I'd never get a reference, and I could forget about getting on to The Scheme, that's for sure. He said this so many times that I also began to worry about not getting on to The Scheme even though I hadn't the slightest bit of interest in it. And I wasn't even thinking about references, I just wanted to get through each day, which would hopefully at some point add up to a month, which would add up to a year, and God knows what would happen after that. Sharif would not have understood that attitude. For him, being a surgeon was everything and he wouldn't have been able to imagine his life any other way. Now he reached over and took my list from me. We were standing at the nurses' station and I was quite relaxed now that the ward round was over, even though my day had barely started and there was a mountain of work to be done. Sharif was quiet as he studied my printout. I was able to observe him as he silently went through the list of patients, making pen marks and ticks next to their names, even crossing a few out despite the fact that they hadn't been discharged yet and weren't even close to it. He seemed to forget that I was there, observing the cut of him, his bright glaring tie, the light brown tweed jacket which he wore every day without exception. It was hard not to feel sorry for the guy. He had been a senior registrar forever. Being a non-national, it didn't matter how much on-call he did or how hard he worked, everyone knew that he had no hope of getting a permanent consultant post here and would have to move down the country somewhere to get one. But he could probably forget about any of the teaching hospitals, and the cut of him now, the slumped shoulders, the distant, worried look seemed to acknowledge this. But then he snapped out of it and stared at me, his nostrils beginning to flare a little, which was always a telltale sign that I was in for it.

    — And in case I forget, he said, don't ever contradict me on the ward round again, OK?

I had no idea what he was referring to. I looked back at him, his intense dark eyes locked on to me.

    — If I say the Hb is eight it's fucking eight OK? And if I say it's twenty-eight then it's twenty-fucking-eight OK?

He stared at me for another moment, then he turned and walked away. As I looked after him I felt none of that pity for him anymore, but rather the immediate and pure hatred that you experience when someone slaps you in the face.

In other words, being a surgical intern was something to be endured and survived, a staging post on the way to other things, but what those things were remained invisible to us and even unimaginable, and all of the likely eventualities were undesirable. You might wonder why we chose this profession to begin with, but we didn't go in for much of that. Too much was directly in front of our faces, too much distracted us from ourselves, our fear mainly, and the long hours of activity and exhaustion, the frenetic days, and especially the endless nights when it seemed that it was just the three of us out of all the people on earth who were awake as the living slept. It was a mark of how removed the night was from the day, how separate and distinct those worlds were, that Stuart and I were now near strangers to each other as we passed each other on the corridor at the heel of our consultant rounds, and that it required a double take before we gave each other the briefest of nods as we stopped to write or check something before continuing on our way, trotting after our teams who would not slow down or wait for us or even notice or care that we had fallen behind.

Of Lynda, however, there was hardly ever any sign, and I only had the odd distant glimpse of her. I anticipated seeing her around every corner, but it seemed that she rarely left the burns unit. On several occasions I found myself in the vicinity of the unit in the hope of catching her and perhaps seeing if she wanted to go for a coffee. But you needed to be buzzed into the burns unit and I had no reason to go into it, as there was zero overlap between general surgery and the plastics service, and Lynch never once received a consult request to go there. I lingered in the cul-de-sac corridor by the entrance pretending to read the advertisements on the noticeboard. But she didn't emerge and I got the impression that she never left the unit other than perhaps to go to radiology to get a scan approved. The radiologists always approved Lynda's requests, and not just because she was an attractive blonde in her twenties and they were leering old men. It was more that she was always clear about why the scans were essential and she always had a response ready to all the radiologists' objections. Someone had overheard one of the plastics consultants say that she was the best intern they'd ever had. Not that it was a surprise to hear that. She was highly organized and the notes she wrote in the patient charts were always immaculate, in handwriting that was pointed and small and slanted slightly to the right and that never deviated or grew in any way ragged even in the dead of night when we were dog-tired and our bodies were screaming out for sleep. On one of my forays to the corridor outside the burns unit I saw her as I stood peering through the window of the unit's door. In the distance she was wearing scrubs even though we hadn't been on call the night before. She was laughing with one of the plastics registrars, and I admit that I felt some jealousy about it. The registrar was a tall person who had been several years ahead of us at university. He was half-Italian and all the women spoke about him in a certain way, even though the running joke was that he wasn't very bright and had apparently been the butt of a lot of practical jokes throughout his college years. But the women in our year laughed, saying that they wouldn't mind that, oh no, they wouldn't mind that at all.

When the last day before the long weekend arrived it turned out that Lynch had cancelled the operating list and the day ended earlier than usual. I hung around the res for a while, and it was strange being there in the daylight with an afternoon sun flooding the kitchen. People were heading off, a few of the SHOs had rented a house in Kerry, and there was palpable good humour about the place. There was no sign of Lynda, and eventually I gave up waiting for her and left the kitchen area and made my way out of the res. I came across Sharif in the consultant car park. He was with one of the SHOs and they seemed to be in a hurry. Sharif stopped when he saw me.

— You should have told us about that man's bloods, he said.

He looked at the SHO, who was also glaring at me.

— The guy with the hernia, Sharif said to me. You should have told us about his labs going off like that.

I had no idea what he was talking about. We had fifty-five in-patients.

— Now we have to go and sort it out, Sharif said. On the Friday of a bank holiday weekend.

They had walked on, but Sharif turned to me and shook his head slowly as if greatly disappointed in me.

— Nice one, he said. Thanks a lot.

I didn't know if I was supposed to follow them or not, but they had already gone in the direction of the emergency exit that led directly into Private 1. The alarm went off as they opened the door as if Sharif's appearance in the hospital was being announced by a fanfare. He would have loved that alright. I started to go after them but then stopped. I got glimpses of Sharif and the SHO as they walked up the corridor but then lost sight of them. It must have been one of the private cases he was referring to. I stood in the same spot for a while before eventually moving away.

I was going home to my parents' house an hour from the city. It was my brother Donal's birthday and I'd bought him the video game he wanted. Just beyond the midpoint of the journey, at the decline in the motorway where you get the first view of the Cooley Mountains and the bay where our town was situated, I realized that I had been driving way above the speed limit and I suddenly grew frightened, slowing down as quickly as possible and moving into the slow lane. I became aware of the pain in my hands from gripping the steering wheel too tightly, but even so it was hard to relax them and I didn't remember having gone through the toll or any other part of the journey, and I slowed my pace so much that it must have taken me another hour to get from there to my parents' house.

I was exhausted when I arrived. I sat on the small sun couch in my parents' kitchen and was blinded by the light that you get there in the north-east in the autumn. It was my first visit home since the start of intern year, and I hadn't seen my parents or anyone outside of work during that three-month spell. I could tell they were worried about me from their silence and the lack of questions and the way my mother wanted to feed me and build me up with red meat and a large fried breakfast. I'd lost weight, they said. Did I not go to the canteen? I wasn't working too hard, was I?

On the Saturday family members came over for Donal's birthday, uncles and aunts, and cousins who were all much younger than me, but I found it difficult to concentrate or engage with any of them, and after the cake was cut and the song was sung I went upstairs to my bedroom and tried to sleep, but every time I closed my eyes I could hear my pager go off, the piercing sound of it so realistic that it seemed to vibrate inside my head. I even got out of bed and on my hands and knees looked on the floor for it, under my pile of clothes, convinced that I had brought it with me by accident. Eventually

I got out of bed again, by which time it was dark outside and all the visitors had gone. My parents and Donal were in the living room watching some celebrity dancing competition on television, and I went out to the kitchen and found some bottles of wine in one of the cabinets. I opened one and drank it quite quickly before opening another one, though I only drank a couple of glasses from the second one. I made sure to hide the empty bottle in the rubbish.

I didn't see Lynda or Stuart until midway through the following week when the roster, after its brief mercy, came back at us with vicious intent. We were to be on twice in four days, two shifts beginning on Tuesday and ending on Saturday morning with only a brief interlude. I hadn't said a word to Sharif since our interaction the previous week and he seemed to pick up on this, even finding it amusing. Whoever that patient with the hernia was and whatever the problem was with his bloods, Sharif never mentioned it again and there was nobody on the census who fit the description. I wasn't going to bring it up and I tried to avoid talking to Sharif at all. But after rounds on the Tuesday I had to ask him for help with a line that I couldn't get in on one of the patients I was supposed to be prepping for theatre. They were already calling for her and I had no choice but to go to Sharif, although I knew it would be futile. Right from my first day the guy had made no effort to help me. On the contrary, he seemed to think that any help he gave me was not in my long-term interest. Instead of actual assistance he liked to give little lectures or pep talks which were practically dripping with nostalgia for his own intern days – 'at The Marsden, "actually",' he always added, to the point where it became a running joke among us. He must have mentioned 'The Marsden, "actually"' two or three times a week, and it was an easy thing for us to make fun of him over. The patient I couldn't get the line in was a young overweight woman with thick arms. She needed the IV as a routine prior to whatever procedure they were doing on her. But for the life of me I couldn't get it in and with each attempt my confidence drained away. The porters had arrived and were waiting in the corridor, loudly complaining about me to the nurse. You mean she's not even ready?! they said. You're telling me the intern's only putting in the IV now?! Jaysus, what's the story, was he out on the piss last night or what? The patient could hear this too. She was a nice person, and she was trying not to show how distressed she was. I must have tried putting the line in six times before giving up and going to Sharif. He was still in Bennetts, sitting at the nurses' station, and as soon as I approached him to ask for his help he sat back, the picture of smugness. So you're talking to me now? he said. He smiled. Perhaps this is a lesson for you, he said, that you should always be collegiate. He leaned back in his chair. Lines were never a problem for him, he said. In fact, at The Marsden it was actually the interns who had had to put in the central ones, long lines they called them there, but also arterial ones, you name it, he said, they were really no problem, once you knew your anatomy. That was the key, he said, you have to picture it in your head, and here he tapped the side of his forehead. I mean *really* picture it, he said, where the basilic breaks off to become the median cubital and then the cephalic, not to mention the median antebrachial, which was always his particular go-to. He was smiling now, this was perhaps his favourite topic of conversation in the world. Meanwhile the clock was ticking and I still had the day-case admissions in Hospital 7 to get to. They must have bleeped me fifteen times. But on and on he went, with another mention of the median antebrachial, which he pronounced with relish, enjoying the harsh syllables on his tongue. Then he got up from his chair and put on his white coat. For a second I thought he was actually going to come with me, but instead he looked at me and said that believe it or not I would actually thank him for this one day. With that, he headed down the corridor to join the others in theatre and left me to it. I don't recall whether I got the line in on the next attempt or if it took me another few goes, but I can still clearly see the woman's face. She was a decent person and she responded to my apologies by saying that no, no, it was OK, really it was OK, but tears were streaming down her cheeks. She was doing her best, but she had lost all belief, all sense of control, in this strange environment in which she had found herself, and she now had absolutely no confidence in what would happen to her.

That evening after work lots of people were hanging about the res, most of them with their coats on and waiting to head over in a group to the pub. A quiz had been organized by the student nurses, and the male doctors in particular were excited about it. Even the female doctors were going to go, if only to watch the boys make arses of themselves, they said. You could tell it was going to be a good night. Lynda, Stuart and I were the only ones in scrubs, condemned to stay behind. The geri's intern was around somewhere also. Her call fell on the same day as ours, but we never saw her and it seemed that she never left her room. Sometimes you could hear music playing from it and once I thought I heard her singing along. The medical intern was about somewhere too, but that was it and otherwise the whole hospital was headed across the road. There was a rumour that Hanratty was going to put in an appearance, perhaps, it was said, to try and score with one of the student nurses, or anyone who'd have him, and we laughed at the prospect. His intern said he had asked her what time proceedings were due to kick off and he had joked that he would be able to answer any of the quiz questions relating to Dire Straits or Manchester City. We all got a good laugh at that as well. The intern was sitting at the long table, the centre of attention. She reached over to stub her cigarette out in the overflowing ashtray. Sad sap, she said, before standing up and putting her coat on. They were all delighted with themselves to be turning their pagers off and escaping from the place, and how we envied them. They left a big silence when they had gone, and it was just the three of us now sitting at the long kitchen table together with a guy called Thomas, a second-year SHO whom I only knew by sight and had never spoken to before. He wanted to let us know about a patient of his who might go off during the night, but the conversation went beyond that and it became clear to me that he was one of those SHOs who loved to hear himself speak with the wise voice of experience. They were always male, these people, and Lynda especially seemed to bring it out in them. I was always surprised to see how much time and space she gave them to impress her. To listen to him go on, you would have thought that Thomas was a senior registrar hardened by years of experience, but he was only a year ahead of us. I remembered him from college as a nerdy type and it was probably the first time in his life that he was in a position of superiority, talking to an attractive woman in this manner. Thomas was telling her about placing a central line, which Lynda hadn't done yet but he had, several times now. He said he'd be happy to show her. The next time there was one that needed doing he'd page her and walk her through it. They're actually fine, he said, once you have your anatomical markings down, they slip right in, and I thought, Christ, not you as well with your anatomical markings. Lynda looked at him and smiled. The conversation moved on to other procedures and Thomas said he'd heard Lynda had put in a chest drain, which was unheard of for an intern. She smiled when she looked at me. Anyway, he was saying now in answer to the question she'd just asked him that no, he wasn't going to go to the student nurses' thing, he was going to go home, and he said it with such confidence, almost disdain at the idea of going to the nurses' thing, that it seemed to me just as likely that nobody had invited him to it. He lived in Harold's Cross, he said in response to another of Lynda's questions. Near to Leinster Road. Above the Spar. Yes, Lynda thought she knew it. I had visions of a bedsit, a miserable night in store. Anyway, he said, getting back to what he had originally wanted to tell us about, he needed to hand over about his patient whom he had admitted earlier that day via casualty, a young African man who was very sick and delirious. Technically he was in under the surgeons because of a minor cellulitis, but the covering consultant was away and therefore he wasn't really under anyone, or at least not in any way other than nominally. It had been down to him to do everything. But when he had gone to the ward to follow up on the patient he had found that none of the orders he'd written in the chart had been carried out. The guy had been left there, the team hadn't done anything. We asked who the intern was, and when he told us we knew the situation right away as that particular individual was renowned for leaving jobs undone so that the on-call people would have to do them. Right now he would be in the thick of the nurses' party, that was his only interest. Thomas said the patient spoke no English and despite the delirium was in no way unkempt or desolate in appearance. What was wrong with him? Lynda asked. He's got some sort of infection, he said. It could be some weird African thing. Something atypical. His immune system seemed to be out of whack totally. He was febrile and having delusions. Thomas had asked for a psych consult but he was pretty sure they would say that it wasn't a primary psych issue but was organic, resulting from the florid infection. We got an interpreter, and you should hear some of the stuff the guy comes out with, Thomas said. He thinks he's Jesus. Maybe he is, I said, but nobody laughed. Anyway, Thomas wanted us to check in on him later on. Any issues, just call the med reg because in fairness it's more of a medical thing than a surgical thing.

I got up and left to throw my stuff into one of the free overnight rooms. I took my time and changed into scrubs, then lay down on the firm bed for a while. I must have slept as I was woken by a knock on the door. Lynda and Stuart were standing there, they were heading over to do the first rounds. I was a bit disorientated and it took me a second to register what they were saying to me. Lynda pointed at my face and laughed. The netting of my bag that I had been using as a pillow had imprinted its meshed pattern on my skin. Both Lynda and Stuart were grinning. I grabbed my white coat and went with them. We walked down the connecting corridor and on to Private 1 just to get it out of the way early. It mainly involved charting a ton of stuff and putting in three lines. One each, Lynda said, but she ended up doing two of them because Stuart couldn't get his one in, and I had more difficulty than usual with mine even though the woman's veins were actually fine. It goes like that with veins. Every time you held someone's arms up to inspect them there was a period of uncertainty about how it would go as each arm represented its own unique puzzle. I apologized to the woman after two unsuccessful goes, but thankfully got it in on the third attempt. Lynda had finished both hers and Stuart's by the time I came out of the room. They were standing at the nurses' station. Stuart was rewriting a kardex, and Lynda, hands in her pockets, was smiling at me. The netting imprint from my bag was still visible on my face apparently. When Stuart had finished, Lynda said that we should go to Bennetts next, she wanted to check in on Jesus.

We were in no rush and went slowly down the long link corridor. It was already pitch dark outside and large sections of the corridor were unlit, the lights out or not switched on, and we walked in silence, pacing ourselves, as we tended to do at the start of any call, but especially now, given how much we were due to be on over the next few days. We were at the starting point of a long march, an endurance test, and it was a comfort to think of it like that, as if the call was only a physical thing and it was simply a matter of perseverance until we came to the end of it. There was no fear and nothing could go wrong, all we had to do was keep our heads down and walk like this for the next three or four days, like nomads marching across a desert, without having to stop to do anything, to intervene or engage. Lynda wanted to know what we were thinking about for dinner, whether we'd do a Chinese or try something else for a change. I was indifferent and Stuart was totally silent. It took us a minute to get it out of him that his mother had made him sandwiches and a flask of tea. Me and Lynda found this hilarious. Another minute passed and she wanted to know if the flask really kept the tea hot for long. She seemed genuinely interested to know the answer.

When we got to Bennetts the nurses were sitting behind the station. They had a long list of jobs for us. Lynda ignored them and asked about the African and they directed us to the last side room on the right. The outside of the door was plastered with isolation signs hung up by infection control, yellow triangles with bright red Xs through them telling us to wash our hands, wear gloves, gowns, even face masks. We ignored the signs and went in and stood around the bed. It was obvious that the guy was very sick. An attendant was sitting in a chair in the corner, a heavily tattooed man in a white uniform. His eyes were closed. Stuart and I stood at the bottom of the bed while Lynda approached the patient and examined him. She was totally absorbed in what she was doing. When she pulled back the sheets the patient didn't flinch. His hospital gown was soaked right through. He turned his head to the side and looked up at her, but he was drowsy and barely conscious. The whites of his eyes were brightly bloodshot and his face was covered with sweat. He was looking beyond us, but then rested his head back on the hard pillow, unperturbed by, and perhaps even unaware of, our presence. He was in a bad way, but as Thomas had mentioned, the guy had been well dressed, whether by himself or someone else – he wasn't unkempt in any way, and his clothes, all brightly coloured, were in a plastic bag in the corner of the room. Lynda pulled the cover back over him. She went over to the sink and washed her hands and we followed her out of the room.

While Lynda wrote her note in the chart Stuart and I answered some of the bleeps that had started to come in. All the wards were looking for us at once, but there was nothing urgent about the things they needed done and they could easily have waited for us to get to them on our rounds. Lynda was taking ages to write her note, and I went across to the nurses' station and peered over her shoulder. She'd written nearly two full pages in her neat blue slanted writing, summarizing in detail her examination findings and the list of investigations needed, ticking the ones that had been done already, which was only about half of them. The list included all of the routine things, but also other things that were not routine. Culture for atypicals. Lumbar puncture. Bone marrow aspirate, biopsy. She had to move me out of the way to get to the printer to print off some of the blood results from the computer and then get back into her chair to sellotape them to the chart. She then finished the note and signed it.

— Come on, I said to her, we need to go, they're getting antsy around the place.

— You two go. He needs a lot done.

— Are you serious?

— Here, take my pager will you?

Stuart was standing beside me with his weighty silence. Lynda was looking at me, her hair tightly pulled back, her blue-green eyes ferocious. I accepted her pager as if it was no big deal.

Stuart and I left Bennetts and headed over to Johns. We walked along a short connecting corridor between the two wards in silence. We each felt Lynda's absence.

Our pace was very slow as if we were giving her time to change her mind and catch up with us. The nurses on Johns knew Stuart well as it was his ward during the day. It was clear that they liked him well enough but also that they considered him ineffectual. Bed 4 spiked, one of them said, he needs a cannula as well, but he's delicate, so why don't we get your friend here to give it a try? Stuart agreed with them instantly, which annoyed me. The list of jobs went all the way to the bottom of the page and the nurses kept adding more things to it. There were no reviews, it was all routine stuff – the cannula and one or two others which needed replacing, a few vanc levels, two sets of cultures, a first dose of antibiotics, and rewriting what seemed like most of the kardexes on the ward.

– Could you not have done half of this stuff during the day? I said to Stuart.

He didn't respond and the two of us stood at the nurses' station in an uneasy silence, rewriting the drug kardexes. We had only finished one when the nurses appeared with another one. Even though I'd just complained about it to Stuart, to me this was actually the preferable part of the job. Everyone complained about doing this sort of menial stuff, but for me it was a relief, a mindless task that you could take refuge in. I would happily have spent the whole night standing there doing that task. I got the same vibe off Stuart, and it was as if we were competing with each other to get the greater part of the work. As soon as he finished one kardex he reached over to take another that was by my side and immediately launched into it. Once we had finished the kardexes we split the other jobs, and that went better than we could have imagined. It could go like this sometimes. Stuart had no bother with the lines and the bloods, and we more or less finished at the same time. It was very satisfying to go through the nurses' jobs list then and cross out all the things we had done.

We left Johns and headed to Duns, where we had both been paged a few times. We stopped at the window outside the ward. It was the one spot in the hospital that gave a decent cityscape, not of the central city, which was a couple of miles away, but of the local area, which was mostly made up of council housing and a large factory. A thick curtain of low clouds were lit up by the lighting underneath. The sky seemed like a permanent fixture, a structural component of the night world that would be long gone and almost inconceivable in the far-off morning, like a dream landscape that your sleeping mind had conjured out of nothing.

On Duns they wanted us to review someone with chest pain, but the patient was asleep. Stuart and I stood at the bottom of the man's bed looking at him, wondering whether to wake him. You could barely make the man out in the darkness, but he seemed peaceful and you could hear a soft, regular snoozing. We went a bit closer to make sure it was coming from him and not the bed next to him on the other side of the curtain. We stood back again, observing the man, wondering what to do.

— What if it's a silent one? Stuart said.

— It's not causing him any bother though.

— Yeah, but how will it look if he's having an MI and we didn't do anything?

— There's no way he's having an MI. He's sleeping like a baby.

Stuart thought about this for a second.

— Yeah, but what if?

I went over and put on the side lamp, hoping that it would accidentally wake the patient, but it didn't, he was totally out of it. A balding middle-aged man, on the obese side, he wasn't even lying flat. He had a tattoo on his temple that seemed decades old. There was no way he was having an MI, but Stuart was right, there was the problem of the chart. We couldn't just write that we didn't assess him because he was asleep.

– I'll go and get the ECG machine, Stuart said.

I nodded at him – in fairness, it was a good idea. When he was gone I took out my stethoscope and listened to the front of the man's chest, another thing I would be able to document in the notes. His light snores came through the diaphragm of the instrument and I switched to the bell. The lungs sounded OK, maybe a bit wheezy, but the truth was I couldn't hear much of anything. I stood back at the bottom of the bed. The man looked perfectly at peace. But it was always a mystery what the body underneath was getting up to, what angry rebellion it was instituting beyond the scope of your awareness. It was an ocean where all sorts of slaughter could be taking place beneath the calm surface. The man was in a deep sleep, but perhaps that just denoted the lack of pain, not the multitude of other ways in which decay or decrepitude announces itself in silence. After a minute I realized I wasn't doing anything except staring at the pattern in the curtain. I was just about to leave when Stuart came back, wheeling the ECG machine. We plugged it in and, picking up the electrode stickers, each did our best to position them on the man's hairy chest. He didn't flinch while we worked on him. When we were finished Stuart stood at the machine and pressed the button and the ECG emerged. We went over and un-clipped the leads, leaving the electrode stickers in place, but they were so badly placed I wondered if we should try and remove them. The next morning the patient's team would look at the location of the stickers and won-der what incompetent fools had been making a mess of the man's ECG. But we left them still attached to the patient and Stuart wheeled the machine out of the ward. We took the ECG over to the nurses' station and bent over it. It looked OK to us. We stapled it into the chart and I wrote the note while Stuart kept seeing things in the pattern of the ECG that didn't exist. It would have been the perfect time to run across Hanratty, and I wondered if he had in fact made it over to the student nurses' party. Eventually I closed over the chart and left it back in the trolley, and the two of us walked off the ward.

It was approaching time to order the food. I didn't have my mobile on me, so I called switch from a phone on the wall at the end of the corridor and asked the woman to connect me to the Chinese takeaway, which she did reluctantly. It wasn't her job to be doing that, she said, but go on, please hold. I ordered the same thing for Lynda that she normally had and something different for myself. They said the food would be there in forty-five minutes. In the meantime we'd be able to cover the two wards between here and the res. Lynda's pager had been going off intermittently. Those calls were mostly intended for any of us, so the nurses were indifferent when I answered instead of Lynda. The exception was the burns unit. When I returned their call, they immediately said, Well, are you coming down to us? and when it was my voice that answered back they were clearly disappointed. They said they had a few jobs but actually it was OK, they weren't urgent and could probably wait for Lynda, when would she be free? Soon, I said. I didn't want to go down there either, so we left it at that.

We went back to Bennetts to tell Lynda about the food. I caught up with her as she was coming out of the storeroom wheeling a trolley. Its lower shelf was packed, a mound of equipment individually wrapped in plastic, several sterile packs. She'd set up for at least one procedure. I looked at the things in more detail and saw that she was going to do an LP and a marrow.

— You doing all that now? I said.

— Who else is going to do it?

— The marrow could be done by the team, no?

— Apparently not.

— Do you need a hand?

— No.

— I ordered some food. We'll be in the res.

She pushed the trolley and we walked together down the corridor until we arrived at the patient's room, where one of the nurses was waiting for her. I could see that the patient was in position, lying over on his side, his bare back visible, the nurse standing there holding him, making sure he didn't fall on to the floor. I held the door open for Lynda and she went in pushing the trolley, allowing the door to close behind her. I stood for a second and then they pulled the curtain across and I turned and went away. At the far end of the corridor Stuart was waiting for me. He hadn't even come on to the ward.

We didn't see Lynda again for the rest of the night. Stuart and I went through both Duns and Willie Wilde wards in record time and found ourselves once more back in the private wing. It was unbelievable how smoothly things were going for us. Even when we went through Private 1 they only wanted us to re-chart a couple of things. So for once we were sitting in the res kitchen waiting for Ed the delivery man to arrive with the food. Stuart had his flask and sandwiches but annoyingly refused to open them until I had my delivery. We sat facing each other at one end of the long table, his mound of sandwiches wrapped carefully in greaseproof paper and the big tartan flask in front of him. If the night continued like this it would be the quietest ever. At last my mobile rang and it was the food. I left Stuart and went down the back corridor and out the rear exit of the res. There was a large stone on the ground and I wedged it into the door to keep it open. It was freezing outside but not raining and the sky above had almost as many stars as you would see if you were in the countryside. I went around the corner and the delivery person was waiting for me. It wasn't Ed this time but a young blonde woman sitting on a motorcycle. I gave her the money and she handed over a plastic bag containing the food. As I walked away she put her helmet back on, then started up the motorbike and headed off.

After we finished eating, Stuart and I both went to our rooms to lie down. I left Lynda's food on the kitchen table, writing her name on the brown paper bag. I was still carrying her pager, but the hospital remained eerily quiet. I kept checking my own to make sure it was working properly, even using the bedside phone to bleep myself. For a long time there wasn't a single bleep, and I lay on the hard bed in the on-call room in an uneasy stillness. Eventually I did get a few calls from various wards, and they came almost as a relief. But nothing was urgent and I asked the nurses to make a list, telling them we'd get to it on our rounds. Stuart would also be getting some of these calls, and I knew that he might get out of bed to go and deal with them. It crossed my mind that he might also end up doing some of the things that I had been called for, but I didn't feel bad about this, especially as I could easily imagine a different scenario, one in which Stuart was right this minute lying in his own bed, not far from where I was, making the exact same calculations as me, and telling whoever paged him to make a list and that he'd get to it when he could. I listened out for the sound of his door opening, his footsteps on the corridor, but there was no sign of this and both of us continued to lie in our respective beds scheming against each other in this manner, a mere fifteen feet between us, as he was in the room just across the hallway from me.

Between the phone calls I must have dozed lightly, experiencing dreams that had a waking quality to them, barely distinguishable from reality. Lynda featured prominently and she was in a bad way, struggling with her patient, who was visibly dying in front of her, and everything that she attempted only made things worse, he was bleeding badly, his blood pressure was in his boots. She was on the phone asking for help even though me and Stuart were also there, but we were no use to her and all I kept saying to her was I don't know I don't know I don't know. It was a relief to be woken by my pager, and even though I dozed again it wasn't long before another call came through, and after a while the trickle of non-urgent calls developed a momentum of their own and I figured it was time to get up. I looked at the small timer on the pager and saw that several hours had passed and that it was nearly morning. I was amazed, jubilant. I sprang out of bed. Stuart's door was shut and I debated knocking on it, but some misplaced sense of decency stopped me. It was only later that I found out he wasn't there anyway. When I passed the kitchen I saw that Lynda's food was still in its paper bag, untouched, and her room, which I passed on the way out of the res, had not been used the entire night, its door was open, the bed still made, her overnight bag on the floor beside it, just as it had been hours earlier. Passing through the connecting corridor, I sensed a change in the air, the stir of morning, birds becoming noisy despite the fact that it was still pitch black outside. I went to the private wing, and to Duns and Wilde wards. They had a few bits and pieces for me, nothing major, and I did whatever was required. I felt pretty good about myself, a sense of pride, the fact that here I was marching around on my own, covering the wards single-handedly for the first time all year. Of course the place was extremely quiet, but still, I felt that I could deal with anything, maybe this was what people meant by experience. I continued going about the wards in this manner until proper daybreak, which I saw evidence of first between Colles and Bennetts, at that strip of window next to the elevators, a gorgeous yellowing sky, swirling clouds that in places revealed behind them a vast clear space, as if something enormous had just been sucked up through it, leaving a rent in the cosmos. I went back to the res and even had time for a shower and a coffee while sitting at the table as the res became busy with people turning up for their day's work. I was there to greet them like a hero, a survivor from the battle of the night which had passed now and over which I had triumphed.

It was Sharif who told me about Lynda. I met him early in the morning for the senior reg rounds. This was a dry round that he liked to do before the 7 a.m. multidisciplinary meeting that took place in radiology. Showered, feeling fresh, for once I was in ahead of him, sitting at the nurses' station with the bloods folder at the ready. He did a double take when he saw me, as generally he was in a foul mood, angry at my being late, and complaining that now we had no choice but to do the dry round on the move as we walked quickly over to the meeting. But this morning he was the one who was a couple of minutes late and here I was waiting for him, the bloods folder open in front of me with not a single piece of data missing in it, I had never been so organized. It was also my job to hunt down all the X-rays of the patients who were up for discussion at the conference. Usually I'd be running around trying to locate them at the last minute, but today I had already pulled them from archives and they were on the floor leaning against my leg. As I went through the list of patients, I noticed Sharif looking at me.

    – I see your girlfriend killed someone during the night, he said.

He was grinning.

    – I met Donoghue, he said. He was called in during the night, they had to take the guy to theatre but he bled out. Apparently she was doing a bone marrow on him. She must have perforated an artery or something.

All I could do was look back at him. The big sneer on his face. He took out his little notebook that he carried everywhere with him. He started to flick through it but then stopped.

— What the fuck was she doing a bone marrow for anyway? he said. The medics do all that crap. We're surgeons for crying out loud.

— Well they didn't, I said. They just left the guy. She had no choice.

He seemed to take what I had said at face value. He went back to his notebook and spent a minute flicking through it before putting it in his back pocket.

— OK, he said. Let's go through the list. Have you got the X-rays for the meeting?

He had to repeat the question before I told him that yes I did.

At the meeting I couldn't concentrate. I sat in my usual spot at the back and had to be prompted when it was my turn to present the five or six patients I was supposed to know about for the meeting. Mr Bailey especially gave me a hard time. He was a short English surgeon who always sat on one of the workstations to the side of the room rather than on a chair like everyone else. On this high perch he would swing his legs like a little boy and take pleasure in acting the contrarian, openly critical of whatever the consensus in the room seemed to be. For each of the patients I presented he picked even more holes than usual in everything, even in the premise of the question our team was asking. *Did we not decide last week that cases like this weren't appropriate for this forum? ... I'm sorry, but did you say this woman is ninety? ... Now why for heaven's sake would you have done that? ... Well what was the white count, I presume you did at least check it? ... Why not a simple plain film of the abdomen before going straight for a CT scan? These tests are very expensive you know ... I'm sorry, but did anyone other than the intern actually examine this patient?* After each of his questions there was only silence and the room's attention fell entirely on me. Neither Professor Lynch nor Sharif said anything, and Mr Bailey kept going on at me, pressing for more information, more detail. *When was her previous surgery? What did they do? Hold on, you said a minute ago she did have a previous hemi, well either she did have it or she didn't have it, which is it? And what about radiotherapy? Why don't you know? I mean, really, is there any point in discussing these cases if we don't have all the information? Tom, do you have anything to add? This is your case again, Tom. Tom?* But Lynch was silent and staring ahead, rigid with anger. Obviously I didn't know the answers to any of Bailey's questions, the patients were all just names on a page to me, the SHOs had told me to add them to the meeting, most of the patients were from outpatients, which I never attended and I doubt if I had ever met any of them, or even if I did it would have been only in passing as they lay in their beds, mute or completely out of it, one of the forty- or fifty-odd we had under us at any one time. At the end of the meeting the lights went on. As we exited I felt a sharp pinch on my elbow and I turned to see that it was Sharif. He came up so close to me I could smell his mouthwash. *That was a disaster*, he said under his breath so that only I could hear him. He was pinching the fold of skin harder so that I let out a little sound of pain. *A ... Fucking ... Disaster*, he said, increasing his grip with each word. And then he let go of my arm and I exited the room along with the rest of the crowd, emerging from the dark room gasping for breath and light. I went in the opposite direction to everyone else and found myself wandering around radiology. I left the department through one of the side doors and came out on to the long corridor. It was full of people and the light was streaming through the windows. It was a different zone entirely from the night before when Lynda, Stuart and I had walked along it. I wasn't sure if it was the light or the exhaustion or the experience at the radiology conference, but I felt dizzy and would happily have lain down on the floor or huddled in the corner. When I got to the end I turned around and went back the way I came. I kept walking, more or less aimlessly, with no idea where I was headed. I found myself back on Bennetts ward, where I had last seen Lynda. It was full of people and action, the usual day-to-day. I didn't expect to see any sign of her and I don't know why I went there. When I stopped outside the room where the African patient had been there was someone else in it and the infection control signage had all been removed, as if the whole thing had never happened. My pager went off and I went over to the nurses' station to answer it. It was Sharif, he wanted to know where I was, they were about to start rounds. I mumbled something about having had to go to radiology, but he had already put the phone down. When I got back to the ward he was with the two SHOs, standing by one of the beds. Sharif stared at me and gave a small shake of the head. We were just wondering what Mr Delaney's

Hb is, he said to me, and I realized then that I didn't have the bloods folder with me. I had no idea where it was. I remembered having it at the conference but had no clue after that. Sharif's face became a stern mask, but other than that he didn't react. For the rest of the round he made a big show of asking for lab results in front of the patients, before saying Oh, that's right, we don't have any lab results today. Sorry, sir, we don't know your blood results, our intern here forgot his folder. Halfway through the rounds Sharif stopped suddenly and said, You know what, this whole thing is pointless without any of the labs, it's just a waste of everyone's time. We'll be having the consultant ward round tomorrow and we'd better have our fucking shit together otherwise Lynch will go ape, but as he said that he was only looking at me. Then both he and the two SHOs headed off to theatre.

The rest of the day was the usual blur of activity. I was pushed along by the nurses' demands and the constant bleeps rather than having any organized list or plan for the day. The bloods folder turned up in the afternoon. One of the student nurses came down on to the ward carrying it. Is this yours? she asked. I was so relieved to see it that I said nothing. She told me she saw it on the ground on the long link corridor and knew straight away that it was mine, as every time she saw me I was carrying it. I had never seen her before and I had never been so grateful towards anyone. I spent the rest of the afternoon getting the folder up to date, and as soon as the activity on the ward calmed down I went to the res and got my stuff. It was already six o'clock, but it felt like I was sneaking out of the hospital early. I cycled home to the house I shared with a group of people from the same town as me. They all worked in technical jobs, for one or other of the multinationals, something to do with semiconductors, computer chips, I had no idea really, especially when they tried to explain to me what they did. One of them worked in a bank, which at least I could more or less understand. I usually only saw them in passing, but that night I went out for a pint with the bank guy. His mother had died recently, a few months back, and even though I knew about it at the time, I hadn't gone to the funeral. I don't think I'd said even anything to him about it. The alcohol went to my head fairly quickly and I kept telling him how sorry I was. He said it was fine, it had been a long time coming and she was sick, but I must have said it fifteen times. I suggested getting one more pint for the road but he said no, perhaps we should head home, he had an early one in the morning. I said I was going to get one anyway and then he said OK, and he stayed with me and had another one, but I sensed his reluctance so I drank it quickly.

The next day was the consultant ward round and Lynch was in foul form, the worst I had seen him since I had started on the team. Sharif bore the brunt of it. Every word he uttered seemed only to antagonize Lynch, who found fault with absolutely everything. Sharif knew not to try and defend himself, and as the ward round continued he became quieter and quieter. He spent the ward round on edge, and then finally the dam burst and Lynch lay into him with a breathless attack that shocked us all with its ferocity. He called Sharif stupid and a fucking fool, and lazy, incompetent, that's what you are, incompetent, you need to get your head out of the sand, boy, you're not in fucking Arabia now you know. He stopped briefly and looked round at each of us before turning back to Sharif and shaking his head at him with pure contempt, almost disgust. We were standing at the end of Bennetts ward. What had set Lynch off was that Sharif had forgotten to book an ICU bed and as a result Friday's long case would have to be cancelled. The ward sister had informed Lynch about it. I'll call them again, Professor, she said, but you know what ICU are like. It's the poor patient I feel sorry for, having their operation cancelled like that. It's a fucking disgrace, Marie, Lynch said, out of breath from his rant, that's what it is, a disgrace. I tell you this much, Marie, and you know this, if that had happened when I was at his level I would have been run out of the place. Old Hennessy would have had my guts for garters. I'd be back working in my father's butchers in Trim. Oh, you're right, Professor, the sister said, you're right.

We left Bennetts to go to some of the other outliers. Lynch stopped and turned to Sharif. Where are we going now? he said gruffly to him. Sharif, whose face had that chastened blood-drained look to it, must have been close to tears. Johns, he said after clearing his throat. We went to Johns and then Duns. Barely a word was said, and we stood in silence in front of the patients we saw there. Whatever updates Sharif provided were given in a low, shaky voice. We were going across the link corridor when we came across Mr Bailey, the short English surgeon, surrounded by his team. Lynch shouted out to him as they approached each other, and the two of them came together like farmers on a country lane. Did you ever hear such shite as that? Lynch said as Bailey approached him. That fucker deserves a kicking, what? Ridiculous. Agreed, Tom, absolutely ridiculous, said Bailey, nodding. But I did warn you, Tom. That's what you get when you put the likes of that in charge. Lynch laughed. Sure they have no clue, he said, they're so disconnected. What do they think we do all day? Anyway, we'll see how it plays out, but fuck me, what? They started whispering to each other and we couldn't make out what was being said and both teams instinctively moved away to leave them to it. I felt a sharp pinch at my elbow, in the exact spot as the previous day. When I turned around Sharif was staring at me, his mouth clenched, his eyes still watering a touch at the corners. He spoke slowly to me, under his breath, seething. Booking the ICU bed is the intern's job, he said. I only do it because you can't handle things. When I was in The Marsden I did *everything*. His grip on my elbow became tighter. EVERYTHING, he repeated. He let go of me and I fell back a bit. The pain was bad and I rubbed my arm. Sharif came up close again. From now on you're on your own, he said, have you got that? You're on your fucking own. I'm going to tell you what to do and you do it, OK? No questions no excuses, I'm sick of it. I'm too good, he said, that's my problem, I'm too fucking good. The two SHOs were off to one side, their faces blank. In that moment I hated them intensely. Just then Stuart's team came on the scene and his consultant joined in the conversation with Lynch and Bailey, with their teams surrounding them, looking on as the three consultants continued with their crude conversation. There was some laughter now, and intermittently they would drop their voices and lean in and say something indecipherable to each other and then laugh some more. I looked over at Stuart, but we didn't make eye contact.

The consultants' little group broke off with a final bout of more raucous laughter, and then the three teams separated and we continued on down the long link corridor to Hospital 7. Lynch was in better form now and the rest of the round was uneventful. There were no more outbursts and Sharif rebounded a little. I was the one who was now silent and vengeful as I rubbed my arm, which hurt badly from whatever way Sharif had grabbed hold of it. But nobody noticed and they didn't speak to me or ask for any lab results. We had a couple of consults down that end of the hospital, two alcoholics who had come in through A & E after vomiting blood, and the question was whether they needed an operation or not. Lynch stood glaring at them from the bottom of the bed, and then we moved away and I wasn't sure what decision had been made or even if there had been one.

After the ward round was over I went to the ICU to see if they could reserve a bed for Friday. But the head nurse was inflexible. You need to put it in the book a week ahead of time, he said. I asked him was there any availability, I told him I was desperate, please I said, almost begging him, but he didn't even check the book and simply repeated that you need to put it in the book a week in advance. There was no point in having rules if people didn't stick to them. I left the unit and went around the corner, stepping into Arnie's stairwell. Even during the day not many people came that way as another stairwell just down from it provided more direct access to ICU and was better lit and had modern automatic doors that were constantly swinging open and closed. Arnie's stairwell didn't have automatic doors and was always in darkness even during the day. But it was like that even before Arnie retreated to it that day. Even fewer people used it now, obviously, and it was almost as if the stairwell didn't lead anywhere, but existed as a stand-alone structure, as if it wasn't connected to anywhere. I closed the door and stood looking over the banister into the silence and the depth, the darkness. The air was cooler than in the rest of the hospital and I pulled my white coat tightly around myself. The ground floor was just about visible. My arm stung badly, Sharif must have burst a capillary in it. I rubbed it and allowed my eyes to water, the tears to gather a little. I looked down into the void trying to imagine the shape of Arnie's broken body at the bottom. I had only ever had a few interactions with him, but I had a good idea of what he was like. He was the last person you'd imagine doing something like that. He was always in good humour and joking and laughing. He got his nickname at college when he started lifting weights in the gym despite being just over five feet tall. He was very popular, and you would look at him and see something to be envious of, what on better days might be worth aiming for. You would marvel at his confidence, his energy, wherever it came from. The day we heard about what happened there was a strange atmosphere in the hospital. We were preparing for our finals then, going around trying to see and examine as many patients as possible. The doctors were going about their day and perhaps we only imagined the vacant look behind their eyes, the mechanical and automatic nature of their movements as they rushed around in silence, hiding their shock at what had happened, already putting it behind them. Arnie lingered in ICU for a few weeks, but nobody visited him apart from his family. We would see them on their way in in the mornings or occasionally in the canteen, but none of us went up to them to say anything or sympathize with them, and then after a while they stopped having to come and that was it. I don't know how long I stayed in the stairwell. My pager went off a few times and I turned it off without checking the number. Eventually I pulled myself away and tidied myself up a bit before pushing open the heavy door and emerging once again on to the main corridor, which was a compressed tube of hospital hustle, uniformed people walking briskly by, talking among themselves. Somehow I was able to get on with the rest of the day and the list of jobs I had to do, but

I didn't talk to or interact with anyone beyond what was strictly necessary.

I didn't run into Stuart until that evening in the res, when we were due to be on call again. He was sitting at the kitchen table reading. I made myself a coffee and sat down across from him, leaning over to see what the book was. *The Screwtape Letters* by C. S. Lewis. He closed it, folding over the corner of the page he was on, and then squeezed it into the already bulging pocket of his white coat. There was a moment of silence between us. I asked him what had happened to Lynda. He looked at me for a second and shook his head. It was terrible, he said, really bad. He didn't know the full story or how the whole thing ended as he'd had to go on his senior reg rounds and by then there was other help on the scene, including Thomas, the SHO who had come in early and who was panicking and losing the head altogether. There was a slight pause where Stuart must have guessed my thoughts. She phoned me, he said, as if he was still surprised about it. She said she needed a hand, quickly, and he had jumped out of bed and practically run over there. She could have called me, I said. Stuart looked at me. There must have been some abnormality of the clotting, he said. It was mad. In the spot on the hip where Lynda had drilled into the chap the blood was gushing out like a geyser, he said, and we couldn't make it stop no matter what we threw at it, pressure, plasma factors, you name it. At one stage I was actually sitting up on his hip, Stuart said, but it was no use. It was mad, the floor was covered with red towels. The guy's BP tanked, his fingers went blue and he was shivering and then he started seizing. The med reg was up and they even had to call Mr Donoghue. When he came in there was war. Effing and blinding, you know the way. Stuart didn't know if the guy died there or in the operating room. God, Lynda must have been freaking out, I said. Not particularly, Stuart said. I mean, yeah, a bit, obviously, he said, but at the same time she kept calm, ran everything, telling me to do this and do that. At one stage she had me running to the blood bank to get more plasma and red cells. She even ran the arrest when the guy started fitting, telling the med reg what to do. I mean, Donoghue gave her a hard time over it, he lost the head altogether after he came in, shouting at her, saying what the fuck did you do, what the fuck did you do, but she spoke calmly back to him. I mean, she tried everything like, *everything*. Shall we say something to her? I asked Stuart. Or maybe we shouldn't bring it up at all, what do you think? I don't know, Stuart said, I don't know, and we left it at that and sat in silence for what felt like a long time and waited for her.

It was a surprise when Rosie the geri's intern came into the kitchen wearing scrubs. She acted as if we were expecting her and sat on the chair next to Stuart. What? she said. You're both looking at me like I've got two heads or something. Where's Lynda? I asked. Sick is what I heard, Rosie said. She gave me a little forced smile. Rosie and I had got together briefly early on in college and it had been awkward between us ever since. Anyway, we were stuck with her, she said, medical admin had asked her to fill in and stupidly she had agreed. She wanted to know the way we did things, did we head over early or did we wait and let things build up? She was looking at Stuart, as if it was up to him. His face went bright red. It occurred to me that they might not know each other. Stuart had gone to a different university than us and they might not have even spoken to each other before now. Yes, Stuart said, which didn't answer her question. Rosie said she'd heard that we didn't divide up the wards, but whatever way we normally did things was fine by her, she'd just fit in. Stuart said yes again and the two of them laughed for some reason. He appeared to be taking the whole thing in his stride and it didn't seem to bother him that Lynda wouldn't be on call with us. If anything, he seemed pleased about it, there was something about his body language, almost a confidence. He stood up and put on his white coat. I just need to go to my room, he said, we can head over then if you are both OK with that. I got myself another coffee and sat down again. Rosie said she'd be back in a minute as well and I was left alone sitting at the long table, looking around at the empty kitchen, every inch of it lit up by the fluorescent tube lights which buzzed slightly. The only other sound was the loud hum of the fridge. After a while, both Rosie and Stuart appeared in the doorway. I stood up and the three of us headed over to the hospital.

Rosie said she hadn't spoken to Lynda directly. It was just the person from medical admin who had contacted her, asking her to swap in to Lynda's call at the last minute. Rosie didn't ask why and admin didn't say anything else to her. They were going to pay her time and a half for stepping in. That's decent of them, Stuart said, and Rosie gave him a playful slap on the shoulder. They were *desperate*, she said, I should have asked for more. Stuart laughed. We were on the long link corridor, we didn't have a firm destination and were walking slowly, Rosie and Stuart ahead of me slightly. I hope she's OK, I said, and they both looked at me like they had no idea what I was talking about. Lynda, I said. Rosie looked back at me and smiled. It was as if she had just confirmed something to herself, something she'd been wondering about.

The night went mostly fine. It was odd having Rosie instead of Lynda. It changed the dynamic, mainly with regard to Stuart. He was more conversant and even took on what you might have called a leadership role. Let's swing by Paddy Duns and then Colles, he said, get them out of the way. They're usually the worst for jobs, he said to Rosie. We followed his lead. Even when it came to the lists of jobs, he took it upon himself to dole them out between the three of us, and he seemed able to get through his tasks well enough. If anything, I was the one who was having trouble, and I had a run of two or three lines in a row which for some reason I couldn't get. I was amazed when Stuart said, Here, let me try, and off he marched in the direction of the supply room. Rosie peered after him as he went down the corridor and then, catching herself, drifted over to the computer. She was doing her medicine rotation at the moment, so surgical internship was new to her. She treated it as if everything was a curious novelty even though it was the same things she had to do, just on different wards. She didn't know any of the nurses and was very polite to them. When the burns unit called us, it was Rosie who suggested that she go down there. Apparently she had never been there and was curious about it. I was staggered when Stuart said that he might accompany her. Here, give us your bleep, he said to me, you might as well go and get some kip.

Rosie was standing beside him, the pair of them looking at me. She seemed pleased with herself. I handed over my bleep and went back to the res. I didn't think I slept but I must have because it seemed like no time at all before the sun was streaming through the window. It was Saturday morning. They had let me sleep through the entire night. I got up and had some coffee and then showered and headed off without talking to the others.

At work the following week there was still no sign of Lynda. We were due to be on call on both the Monday and the Thursday, and in between this my day job was inordinately busy, more so than usual. Lynch's list that had been postponed the previous week was added on to this week's one. We had patients all over the place. Half the ones in Hospital 7, the five-day ward, belonged to us and they were calling me every five minutes. They all needed to be admitted urgently, have their bloods and IV lines done, be consented for procedures that I didn't fully comprehend, ECGs, physio referrals, the HDU bed booked, their scans hunted down and the packet sent on with them as they headed off to the operating theatre. Invariably there would be some last-minute hitch, a heart murmur that needed cardiology assessment, a sore tooth, a skin rash, an infected ear, you name it, one of them had it, all of which meant that I had to organize other things for them, and everything was urgent – the dentist who was impossible to get hold of, dermatology, ENT – and all the time the team in theatre had no choice but to wait and wait and wait. Sharif sent down the two SHOs to see what the delay was. They asked me what the problem was and I showed them my list of jobs which stretched to two pages. The girl made a show of studying it while the guy stood there looking around him as if none of this had anything to do with him. She handed me back the list and said that I really needed to hurry, Sharif was going ballistic up there and Lynch would be arriving any minute expecting to get started. He'll go ape, she said, he might not give you a reference over it. Here, she said, pointing at the list. Do these ones next so that we can get started on them at least. Leave the oesophagus and the stomach until the end because we won't be doing those until the afternoon anyway. Then they headed back upstairs, leaving me with the list of jobs that all the time was growing. Even as I was standing there listening to her, my pager was going off. The rest of the hospital was looking for me, because in addition to all of this elective stuff there were also several sick patients around the place, people in various stages of recovery from their operations, or of non-recovery, which is what it looked like to me most of the time, and the nurses needed them reviewed or their kardexes rewritten or first- or second-dose antibiotics given or their urinary catheter changed or their lines replaced or their Hickman line bloods drawn or their warfarin charted or cultures taken, both peripheral and central. One of the patients in particular needed a lot done. His had been a combined operation between Lynch and Stuart's consultant. Between them they'd removed half the guy's face and neck to get at the tumour in his throat. Afterwards he developed a fistula, an abnormal connection between two of his organs. This was what the surgeons feared perhaps more than anything else, they would use the term almost reverentially on ward rounds, and it was the first thing they thought of if someone wasn't recovering the way they were supposed to. As soon as it was mentioned they had to go looking for it, with more tests and more procedures. This particular patient had developed a fistula between his oesophagus and his outer skin. If he ate anything the contents would appear on his chest wall, so we hadn't let him eat anything for weeks. He had been lying there ever since I started with the Lynch team, his throat dry and raspy when he spoke, wasting away in a side room despite, or perhaps because of, the several tubes and lines that were either draining him or feeding him, as well as others which kept his pain under control, with his family constantly surrounding him, wanting more things done, wanting to talk to someone, the nurses telling them that they'd paged the intern several times already but he wasn't answering, he never answers, that fella, we don't know where he is half the time. It was only much later, towards the end of the morning, after the theatre list was more or less done, that I could finally make it back up to the ward, where the nurses gave me plenty of attitude. Oh here he is now, the ward sister said, so good of you to join us. We had to get your colleague here to talk to that family for you, and there was Stuart sitting behind the desk looking bashful and embarrassed but also smug at the same time.

I thought Sharif would be furious with me because of all the delays in getting the patients to theatre that morning. But when I saw him later in the evening for the post-op rounds he was in great form. Apparently they had had to borrow extra theatre space from Mr Bailey's list and Sharif told me Lynch had been delighted about this small victory over his colleague. We should do this every week, Sharif said. He said he had to shuttle between the two operating theatres, it was amazing, the place was humming, a well-oiled surgical machine he called it, proper surgery, it reminded him of The Marsden actually. The SHOs had to step up he said, it was great for their training man, great, like a war zone, which by the way if you ever get a chance to go to one you should grab it, it is the best opportunity for learning to cut. It was one of his major regrets that he never got a chance to do so, military service in his country was nothing you see, absolutely nothing, just exercises man, it was like the boy scouts, there had been no good wars. He was still in his scrubs and he sat back against the chair at the nurses' station. I'd never seen him as pleased with himself. An exhausted glow emanated from him – possibly it was the happiest moment of his life, definitely in the top ten. By that stage I was drained. I wanted to go home and not talk to anyone and fall asleep or at least lie there motionless staring into the darkness. But after the rounds were over, as I was passing through the res to go home, I saw Stuart dressed in scrubs. He saw me with my bag on my back heading out the door and the look on his face seemed to be asking me where did I think I was off to? I walked over to check the schedule which was typed out on a sheet of paper hanging above the microwave. There were many edits and pen marks on it, but you could still make out clearly that it was indeed this night we were on, not the next one as I had thought. All I wanted was to get out of the place, but instead I turned without saying another word and went to my usual room in the res and put my bag on the floor and stayed there sitting on the bed for ages with my head in my hands. It was a long time before I finally summoned up the will to go back into the kitchen. Rosie was there, she was covering for Lynda again. She and Stuart were sitting next to each other at the long table. Their conversation stopped when I appeared. Stuart's face was flushed red. Rosie said hello to me, but she was smiling, almost laughing.

Almost immediately our pagers started to go off and it seemed that they never stopped. We had no choice but to divide the wards up and go our separate ways. It was the middle of the night before there was a brief lull and the three of us met by chance on the long link corridor at the turn-off for radiology. Up until that point it had been relentless, as if the hospital at night was rebelling against its daytime counterpart, objecting to the burden those earlier hours of activity had placed on it. There was too much pain, too much suffering, too many broken bodies for it to deal with, scattered around the place. Right from the first crop of bleeps we were behind in our work, and it wasn't just the routine stuff. There were a bunch of sickies and they all seemed to be going off at once. Remarkably, it had been Stuart's suggestion to divide up the wards and go our separate ways. Rosie backed him immediately and I was the one who was hesitant about it. The name of one of the sickies was familiar to me. Rosie got the bleep, but apparently the man was a Lynch patient, he was down in Hospital 7 recovering from his operation, so it was agreed that I should head in that direction. I half jogged down the long link corridor and then past the burns unit, whose frosted window I stopped at briefly out of habit to peer through. There was nothing much to see – the corridor leading to the nurses' station, one of the attendants walking by pushing a trolley. It occurred to me that the staff there might have heard from Lynda, but I didn't follow up on that thought. I went past casualty, the automatic door of the ambulance bay opening as I went by, creating a zone of cold air. Another corridor led to Hospital 7, which was similar to Hospital 5 in that it was a far older building which had been absorbed into the more modern main campus, and it was similarly more like a priest's home than a hospital, the air thick with silence, the slightest sound echoing off its polished tiled floors. I was met by one of the nurses, who was clearly concerned about her patient. He's not been right since he came back from theatre, she said, and she led me down the corridor to where the patient's bed was. The man didn't look in any way familiar to me, and I would have denied having had anything to do with him were it not for the fact that it was my own handwriting in the chart from earlier in the day when I had admitted him and got him ready for theatre. But it might as well have been from years earlier or even from some point in the future, I had no recollection of it. My own words struck me as amazing in their self-confidence, pronouncing the man fine and fit for the operation, the physical examination was NAD, I had written in large capitals, Nothing Abnormal Detected. He was the one who had needed the cardiology assessment, and I was relieved that I had at least arranged that much for him before sending him off to the operating room. I looked at the nurse. He would have also been assessed by the anaesthetist, I said to her. She didn't say anything. I stood at the bottom of the bed and looked at the man as he writhed in pain, he seemed to be in a bad way. I did an ECG, the nurse said, and I looked at her. We have our own machine here, she said, I know how to work it, it's easy, I left the printout in the office. I turned back to the patient and both of us stood looking at him. Will I give him some morphine? the nurse asked. I looked back at her for a second. Yes, I said. She had already drawn up some in a syringe and got me to check it with her and sign her log book. I stood at the side of the bed and tried to feel the patient's abdomen, but I couldn't even put my hand on his skin he was writhing around so much, so I told the nurse to go ahead with the injection. I tried asking the man some questions. Had this sort of thing ever happened to him before? What brought it on? Were there any relieving or exacerbating factors? Any family history? Any drug allergies? But he was in another world and the questions felt ridiculous, he didn't respond to me except in groans, but even these were cut off by his gaspy little breaths. I stood for a while, I don't know how long, looking down at him as the nurse went off to get a morphine refill in case we needed more of it. I was very worried but gradually felt calmer, and then I realized it was because the man himself had started to calm down. His breathing was deeper and when the nurse came back it had developed into a small snoring sound. I pressed gently on his abdomen, and it was now soft and fat, still damp with sweat. He seems grand now, said the nurse. I'll have to get rid of this, she said about the syringe she was holding. Maybe we could split it, I said, and she looked at me for a second and we both laughed. God knows what was wrong with him, I said, and the pair of us stood looking down on the man for a few moments. We then turned and left the room and walked back to the nurses' station. Here, the nurse said, handing me the ECG she had taken. I took it and studied it for a while. The rate was fast but there was nothing too abnormal about it. Although one of the leads possibly had a bit of T-wave inversion. I pointed that out to the nurse and she looked at it but appeared dubious. Looks OK to me, she said, and I knew she was right, the ECG was fine, certainly nothing obvious on it. I saw the sign for echocardiography, which was just across the corridor from Hospital 7. It made me think of Hanratty. I laughed. Well, if there was any doubt, we could always knock on the echo room door and get a cardiology consult. The nurse looked back at me. I told her that Dr Hanratty, one of the cardiology consultants, sleeps there believe it or not, in the actual echo room. I laughed again, but the nurse didn't react and her manner changed. She asked me had I not heard. Heard what? She looked around to make sure nobody was listening. He took his own life last week, she said. No, I hadn't heard that. I was silent. He went to a hotel, she said. That's what the girls were saying, you know that hotel out near the airport? The same one those doctors went to last year that were in the news, the ones who had made the pact. One of the girls is flatmates with one of the cardiac technicians. Apparently he had told everyone he was going to get some sun. They found him the next morning. He had taken insulin and something else, one of those anaesthetic drugs. We were in the little office now and I sat on a seat and rested back against the wall. The nurse thought she heard something, one of the patient alarms, and she headed off. From where I was sitting I could see the sign for cardiology. For a moment I lost track of time. There was a mechanical hum and it took me a while to work out that it was coming from the small electrical heater. The nurse came back into the room and told me not to get too comfortable, that she had another few jobs for me, three cannulas as it turned out and a couple of first-dose antibiotics. She paused and looked at me. Are you OK? she asked and I told her yes and stood up. I did the jobs and rewrote a few kardexes, charted a few other things, but I moved slowly, automatically. I barely knew what I was doing and I tried not to think of Dr Hanratty. The nurse was very helpful, getting some of the equipment together for the lines and even priming the lines with the antibiotics for me. She was as young as I was but she seemed more experienced and competent in her job. Her attitude rubbed off on me and I noticed that it seemed to help me. The lines were no problem, for example, and I did everything on her list without thinking about it and had no memory afterwards of any of the tasks, just the awareness that I'd been on the ward for a good while. After I finished I headed back to the main hospital, surprised once more by the cold air from the ambulance bay as I passed by. They were bringing someone in on a stretcher, it was a woman in an oxygen mask with blonde hair. It wasn't clear what age she was and I thought it might be someone young, someone in their twenties. I stopped still and stared at the figure on the trolley, the hair hanging down over the sides. I had the urge to move closer but also to run away. When the paramedics passed by with her just in front of me I saw with relief that it wasn't Lynda, rather a woman in her sixties or even seventies and I could tell that she had been chronically unwell and was unkempt. I even laughed at the idea of Lynda's reaction were she to think I had confused her with this old, dishevelled woman. Again I paused at the burns unit and looked through the small window of the door leading to it. There was nothing to see and the lights had been dimmed. I continued on until I reached the long link corridor, and this is where I came across Stuart and Rosie. They were laughing and didn't see me at first and I felt that I was interrupting something between them when I came upon them. The three of us then walked along the corridor together. The sense of ease I had felt in Hospital 7 had vanished and I was now exhausted, I had pain behind my eyes and a headache and my throat was dry. I could have happily lain down on the floor and slept. I thought there was a fair chance that Stuart and Rosie would want to get rid of me, and I was hoping for this, but still the bleeps kept coming and we didn't have time to order food and it was going to be too late for that now anyway. I took a bunch of the packs of plain biscuits meant for the patients out of a cardboard box, and later, when we had finally made it back to the res, I ate about ten packs to go with the five or six cups of industrial-strength coffee that I must have drunk. Stuart and Rosie sat in the living room. They both had a packed lunch, possibly they shared Stuart's one. I stayed on my own in the kitchen, sitting at the long table, listening to the murmur of their conversation which I couldn't make out. It was mostly Rosie talking, but Stuart was also doing his fair share, his deep northern tones thrumming out bass notes which seemed to come through the wall. I was too tired to make my way to the bedroom, and then the lull ended and our pagers started going off, my one first and then from the other room, in quick succession, either Stuart's or Rosie's. It was the nurse from Hospital 7. That man's gone off again, she said, you'd better hurry. The panic in her voice was frightening considering how in control I knew her to be. Just then Rosie came out into the kitchen, Stuart behind her. It turned out she was also carrying the arrest bleep that night. A voice was coming out of it. *Cardiac Arrest Hospital 7. Room 4 Bed 2. Cardiac Arrest Hospital 7. Room 4 Bed 2.* Rosie and Stuart were looking at me. You were just there, Rosie said, and from the way she said it and the way they were looking at me it felt like they were accusing me of something. The three of us hurried out of the res and across to the main corridor. We went through Private 1 and the nurses said good, we were just about to call you, but we ignored them and continued past quickly. None of us spoke and I followed along behind the two others, who were striding more purposefully. The cold air from the ambulance bay was refreshing but maddeningly brief. The automatic doors closed as we passed by and it seemed that the outcome of something had been decided. When we arrived at Hospital 7 there was a commotion at the far end. A stretcher was parked outside the patient's room and a couple of bedside chairs had been pushed out into the corridor. The light was on and loud voices were coming from the room. Our pace slowed. Approaching the room was like approaching the mouth of a cave containing some primitive but unspecified danger. When we entered the room where all the activity was, it was clear that we weren't needed. A crowd was around the patient's bed – the arrest team were performing CPR. The curtains around the other patients' beds had been pulled around them, although it would have been impossible for anyone to sleep through all the commotion. I got a glimpse of an elderly man sitting on the edge of his bed in the semi-darkness, staring at the ground as if wondering whether it would be his turn next. The nurse who had helped me earlier was in the middle of things. She wasn't leading the arrest but was helping to get various items from the crash trolley, with the same quiet efficiency I'd noticed before. She seemed to anticipate whatever was needed next. The med reg was running the arrest. She was standing back a bit, talking

to the person next to her, another nurse who I also recognized, someone older who was permanently attached
to the arrest team and had taught a short CPR course to
us during our induction at the start of the year. The person performing the compressions did so in time with her
own loud counting. One and Two and Three and Four
and Five and Six and Seven ... The arrest went on for a
while, the team stopping every now and again to check
for a rhythm on the defib monitor. Asystole, the med reg
said each time, leaning over to look at the screen. She
threw the oxygen mask up in the air and caught it. Continue on, she said, let's give it another few minutes, he's
young enough. I wanted them to continue for ever, but
at the same time I saw that the whole thing was pointless. I thought Stuart and Rosie were still beside me, but
then I noticed Stuart at the patient's wrist, he was trying
to get a blood gas. Rosie was standing behind the person
doing compressions ready to take a turn, asking her if
she needed a rest. But before they changed places the
med reg asked the nurse beside her what time it was and
after a moment's pause said, Right, that's it folks, let's
call it. Time of death three forty.

Afterwards the three of us walked back up the long
link corridor. A calm elation emanated from Rosie and
Stuart, some residual adrenaline from what they had

just experienced, taken part in, the physical exertion of it, a sense of satisfaction that they had not looked or felt out of place, and acceptance that the result itself was irrelevant to this feeling. The silence between us was an acknowledgement of this. Behind this, though, was another silence which was of a different character, it was judgemental, even accusatory, and I alone was enveloped by it. The other two didn't say anything or ask me anything about the time earlier in the evening when I had reviewed the man. They didn't speculate about what it was I must have missed, because surely I had missed something, and the fact that they withheld any such comments only made it worse. When we got to the stairwell at Private 1 Rosie said we should go through it properly rather than avoid it because we knew already that they were looking for us and they'd only call us later. I followed after her and Stuart, and we stopped at the nurses' station. Sure enough, there was a long list of things for us to do, but no reviews and nobody sick, it was just routine jobs. I found it hard to summon the will to move from the spot I was standing in. Rosie was dividing up the jobs three ways, but Stuart turned to me and said, You look wrecked man, why don't you hit the hay. It was only later, maybe even the next day or the next week, that it occurred to me that I never thanked him or said anything at all to them. Instead I walked away down the carpeted ward and through the connecting corridor, that unearthly space passageway that was like a vacuum between two worlds, to the rest of the night.

The next day nothing was said about the man who had died. I kept waiting for someone to mention it to me, for it to come up in some other, perhaps more official way, a phone call from medical admin or a summons to the Prof of Surgery's office, but at the same time I knew that these things wouldn't happen and that it would pass like everything else and be folded into what was forgotten. There was always the chance that in the coming weeks the case would be on for the Death Conference, a step-by-step review of what was done and what was not done. But that would be the entirety of it, and all I had was the unease which I knew would follow me everywhere for the foreseeable future, though probably not forever, and which was part guilt and part acquiescence to the way of things, with nothing that would resolve it definitively in either direction. Sharif didn't even seem to notice that one of his patients, whom he had operated on the day before, had disappeared from the census. I tried to tell him about it and even to bring up my own inglorious involvement in it, but he wasn't interested. As long as it had nothing to do with the surgery, he said. And he knew for a fact that it didn't. That anastomosis

I did on him was pristine, man. Priss. Teen. The guy could have no complaints. I'm telling you my friend, it was textbook. You could make an instructional video out of it and put it on the Internet. If it was a heart thing, then that's on the anaesthetist or the cardiology guys, I'm a surgeon. You know what, sometimes these patients can't take it, a surgery like that. They haven't looked after themselves. They're overweight. Drink too much. Smoke too much. Wrecks. It's like putting a Ferrari engine into an old banger. No disrespect to the guy. We walked on, heading to the private wards to finish the rest of the round. Sharif paid some attention to my reaction because his tone changed a little. Look, he said, turning around to me. Sometimes people die dude. Simple as. He gave a big shrug and went back to interacting with the SHOs. He was still buzzing from the day before. *Five majors and* how *many minors?* he kept repeating as we made our way around the hospital on our ward round. Eleven, one of the SHOs would say, to which he would reply, Eleven? Did you say *eleven*? Wow, I'm good, I'm good. He kept telling the SHOs that they finally knew what a high-functioning surgical unit looked like, that their hands must be aching, right, and their shoulders and their neck muscles must be stiff, right, and they must have slept like babies, right, go on, admit it, this is real surgery, there's nothing better man, nothing in this world. He didn't get much reaction and the female SHO gave her boyfriend a few glances, but she didn't look at Sharif with the same contempt that she normally did and she was mostly laughing along with him. After the rounds were over I walked around the hospital in a daze. Nothing seemed to be quite real, it was as if the hospital was covered in a layer of cling film and nothing underneath it was properly functional and everything existed just on the surface. None of the machines did anything and the uniforms everyone was wearing were just costumes. The nurses had to repeat things to me and I had trouble understanding the simplest things that they wanted me to do. I was able to get through each of the jobs on my list because the majority of them were mindless tasks. I left the tourniquet on a patient after putting in an IV cannula on him and the man had to call me back. He was politely pointing at his arm, blood streaming down it, but even then I just looked at him not understanding what the problem was and why on earth there was blood streaming down his skin, forming a bright red expanding stain on the white sheet. On the evening ward round Sharif finally noticed. Dude what's wrong with you? he said, and I had no answer for him. Then he surprised me by asking where's your girlfriend by the way? I haven't seen her around since she killed that guy. He let out a little laugh. Has anyone checked on her, he said, to make sure she's not hanging from the rafters? He laughed again as if he had told a good one and I continued to look at him blankly. I told him that I didn't know and as far as I knew nobody had checked on her.

Sharif's high spirits didn't last long and by the following morning he was back to his usual self. We met at seven for the dry round and when I arrived he was already waiting for me behind the nurses' station in Bennetts. The ward sister was having her own meeting at the other end of the desk, surrounded by the nurses and student nurses. Sharif looked tired. He was in scrubs but wore his tweed jacket over them. As I went through the list of patients he was barely listening, and the ward sister's voice dominated the area. She was scolding one of the student nurses for a piece of jewellery she was wearing, and another one for coming in late. It took us a while to notice that Therese, one of our long-stay patients, had approached the nurses' area and had been standing there for I don't know how long. A tall, skeletal figure, she had her hand on the IV stand and her TPN feed was hanging from it.

– The machine is beeping, she said.

But she might as well have been speaking to herself. The nurses' discussion continued and Therese had to speak louder.

– The machine is beeping, she said again.

One or two of the nurses looked back but none of them said anything.

– CAN SOMEONE PLEASE HELP ME? Therese shouted.

Everyone was looking at her now. She was a striking sight, her pink dressing gown ludicrously small for her. She looked like a mad visionary as she stood there gripping the IV stand like a staff.

– Can you make it stop? she said. It's been like that all night, I can't take it any more.

The ward sister was looking at her with pure contempt. After a long, tense moment she finally spoke to Therese, barely able to control her anger.

– Get back to your bed, she said. Someone will be down to you presently.

Therese turned away but became upset as she walked off pushing her still-beeping IV stand ahead of her.

— I do exist you know! she shouted back. I've every right to be here, it's not my fault I'm bleedin' sick.

There was silence at the other end of the nurses' station, and then a chair was pushed back angrily. The ward sister was now standing over Sharif.

— You need to do something about bed 5, she said to him.

Sharif looked up at her from his seat, taken aback by her tone. The nurses were all looking at us. The ward sister was a glamorous older woman with a slight northern tinge to her accent. The rumour was that she and Lynch had been having an affair for years.

— I mean it, Sharif, she said, this is beyond ridiculous. If you can't sort it out I'll talk to Professor Lynch and he'll have to get involved. And we both know he won't be too happy about that, now, don't we?

Sharif looked up at her, his face suffused with colour.

— Yes Sister, Sharif said, and the sister went back to her seat.

— Now, where were we? she said to the other nurses.

Sharif was rigid with a fury that was indistinguishable from his humiliation. It was bad enough to have Lynch talk to him like that in front of everybody. He sat still, every muscle in his body tense. The sleepiness that was in him had completely evaporated. I waited a moment before continuing with the list, but he interrupted me.

— I want you to get that one a scan, he said. Then I want her transferred off our list. OK?

I reminded him that she'd had a scan recently and it didn't show anything, but this made him more angry and he shook his head slowly.

— Just get it done.

— What will I put on the form?

— I don't fucking care, he said. Christ. Just say query lymphoma, or one of those other things.

I thought for a minute, but this only seemed to frustrate him.

— Look, he said. I shouldn't even be dealing with this crap. Do you think the senior surgical registrar at The Marsden is going around sorting out psych patients? The house staff do all that nonsense. He just comes in and out to cut. In other words, this is supposed to be *your* job. Deal with it. I'm a fucking surgeon for Christ sake!

He stood up.

— Just take care of it OK? I'm sick of taking shit because of you. From one end of the day to the other. Sick of it. It's like a fucking kindergarten around here half the time.

The nurses were all listening to what Sharif was saying. He walked away but then stopped and stood in front of them before turning to shout back at me one more time.

— I mean it, he said. Sister is right. I want that patient scanned and transferred to the medics or the psych team. There's zero surgical going on with her.

So make it happen. By the end of the day. Just get it done.

Then he was gone and all the nurses were looking at me now, and it took a minute for their conversation to go back to the level it had been at before.

Therese was sitting on the side of her bed when I went to her. The curtain was drawn around the bed and she was staring at the space in front of her. Her IV machine was still beeping, but only intermittently, as if it was aware that it had got her into trouble. I looked at the control panel and pressed the flashing alarm button on it.

— I already tried that, she said.

I pressed it another few times then sat down on the edge of the bed beside her. Neither of us said anything. The machine beeped another couple of times.

— Maybe it's trying to communicate with us, I said.

Therese gave a little laugh.

— Well it could tell some bleedin' story, she said, that's for sure.

— Can you imagine? I said. The things it could come
out with, the stuff it has witnessed down the years.

— Ha! she said. It would be no bleedin' comedy
anyway.

— More of a farce, I said, and she seemed to like
that.

— Monty bleedin' Python, she said.

We sat in silence for a moment.

— Listen, I said, the way we beat that ward sister
is for us to make you better, to get you out of here
looking a million dollars.

— I'm trying, Therese said.

— It's not your fault, I said, it's ours. We're not smart
enough to figure out what's wrong with you.

— Yeah well, it's like they're not even trying, she said.
That Professor Lynch, he just walks right past me,
it's like I don't exist.

– I wouldn't mind him, I said, he's like that with me too.

She seemed to find that funny.

– Yeah, I noticed, she said.

– Listen, I said, I'm going to try and get you transferred to the medics, you'll be better off under them.

I stood up.

– I'll pop back later to do your bloods.

Therese nodded.

– Thanks, she said.

Radiology didn't open until nine but I headed down there to get Therese's old films from archives. Arranging a scan for someone was not straightforward even when it was plainly necessary, so I didn't know how I was going to organize one for Therese. There was only one machine and the radiographers all took their breaks at the same time, meaning that the slots were limited. Getting the scan required the approval of one of the consultant radiologists and sometimes they wanted the patient's old films to look at and sometimes they didn't. In Therese's case it probably wasn't necessary. Everyone knew her, she'd been in here since well before I had started with the Lynch team. She had presented one night on surgical take with unexplained weight loss and the on-call surgical SHO got in big trouble with Lynch the next day for having admitted her under him. Apparently Lynch swore that that particular SHO would never get a job in this hospital. But we were stuck with Therese. None of the investigations ever showed anything and the consensus was that it was all in her head. But she clearly wasn't well, she was skin and bones and reported being in constant pain. Nevertheless, even if it isn't just in her head, Sharif maintained, there was zero surgical going on with her, and he was probably correct about that. She should be under the medics, not us, he said, let them sort her out. This attitude had spread to the nurses on our ward, especially the ward sister, who had no patience for malingerers and time wasters, terms she applied liberally to just about anyone who wasn't having an acute surgical emergency or in a well-paced recovery from one. Therese had more 'abdominal pain' last night, she would say at the nurses' report, rolling her eyes and causing the other nurses to laugh. The consensus now was that she might even be faking her symptoms, or at the very least contributing to them. Munchausen's was mentioned. Some of the nurses reported seeing her trying to make herself sick or alternatively eating when nobody was looking. When she developed cellulitis around an IV site it was because she had been rooting around in it, picking at it, possibly introducing feculent matter into the wound. I was the only one on our team who had any interaction with her, mainly because it fell to me to take her bloods. She had a Hickman catheter and the phlebotomist didn't have her certificate for taking blood from it. Neither did I, of course, but that didn't seem to matter to anyone. So each day I had to clean the line from the point where it emerged from her chest wall and fill the little tubes with blood. I got the impression that she looked forward to my visits. The pain was bad last night, she'd say, could they not increase the patch, give her another anti-sickness? Our conversations were also how she found out about what the immediate future held for her. Are they planning to do any X-rays? she always wanted to know, and I liked that she never seemed to be including me when she said 'they'. Christ, I hope I don't have to drink that stuff again, I'll puke my ring up. I told her not to worry, there were no tests planned. We hadn't done any in weeks and probably wouldn't be doing any at all. It was as if the hospital had lost interest in her and the only tests we ever did were the daily bloods, but I was the only one who looked at the results, and if I stopped doing them nobody would have noticed. In other words, the woman existed in total limbo. She couldn't be discharged, but neither could she be cured. And though she was clearly sick, she wasn't sick enough. She was in a make-believe hospital playing the part of a make-believe patient, with no treatments and no tests and no end in sight, and it seemed inevitable that she would die here. The only question was how many months or even years that would take.

The archive room was at the far end of the radiology department. It was an enormous space filled with plastic packets containing large cardboard envelopes which overfilled the shelving units stacked all the way to the ceiling. Each unit was crammed with these packets and the shelving units seemed to groan under their weight. I turned on the back lights and more rows came into view, stretching all the way to the rear of the room, where some of the lights had given out. Supposedly every X-ray and scan that had ever been performed in the hospital was contained in this storeroom. The plan was to digitize everything to make it compatible with the new online PACS system they were bringing in. But here, at least for now, were the hospital's memory banks in physical form, containing a visual snapshot of every patient who had ever passed through its doors, or at least of all those who had had any type of X-ray taken, which would have been the vast majority of course, as it is almost impossible to be admitted to hospital and not to have some sort of X-ray taken. The room was the visual record of their existence, it vouched for whatever had brought them here. The thickness of each envelope told you something of their story, the more bulging ones suggesting prolonged or recurrent stays at the hospital, with chronic ill health and multiple admissions, whereas the slimmer packets reflected some momentary isolated event, a freshly fractured bone perhaps, displaced or avulsed by some unrecorded trauma. Whole families were contained in this room, though they didn't lie alongside each other like in a graveyard. Their bones similarly persisted, but here also were their lungs, their abdomens, their hearts and their brains, damaged but on the whole still pristine. You could find their stomachs if you wanted to, or their duodenums, their jejuna, their ilea, captured in the stark relief of white barium contrast or gastrografin against the misty contours of their bowel loops. Their enhanced livers were still engorged by blood, gadolinium lit. Their brains were still bleeding or infarcted, their kidneys bloated or blocked. Angiograms revealed their arteries to be narrowed, wiry against the pale grey.

Therese's scans were located in the row indicated by the last two digits of her medical record number. From there it went by year of birth, then month, then day. It didn't take long to locate them on the uppermost shelf. I used the wheeled ladder to retrieve them. The weight of her packet was significant – there must have been five hundred sheets of film inside. I took out one to verify that the contents matched the date of her most recent CT scan, written on the outer envelope. It displayed her unhappy thin body when I held it to the light, a series of tiny cross-sectional images arranged in six × eight rows of 5mm slices.

The radiology department was just opening. The grille over the reception area was only half up, but some of the secretaries were already at their desks. I went in through the back entrance to find the consultant roster. Two secretaries were chatting, both of them holding enormous coffees. It's not nine o'clock yet, one of them said to me, but I ignored her and went over to the wall where the roster was hung up. I said it's not nine o'clock yet, the secretary said again, and she and her friend shook their heads. They hated interns down here, we were like pests that needed to be eliminated. The second any of us ventured into the department we were in the way. From their point of view we were the embodiment of more work being imposed on them, because it was us who brought the request forms for whatever scan or test we were trying to arrange. The secretaries acted as the initial gatekeepers and they relished the role, perched on high stools by the front window, taking their time to acknowledge our presence when we appeared behind them. They refused to book anything on the computer unless our form was signed by one of the consultant radiologists, whom we would then have to track down to whatever dark room or office they were holed up in and make something like a sales pitch to them, their default inclination being to turn everything down. Half the time we didn't know what to say, we were just following the orders of our own consultants or registrars, and they rarely let us in on their thinking, they just wanted us to make it happen, whatever it was, to arrange the CT or MRI scan, the ultrasound or barium study, but they never told us why. The roster said that McClean was in Ultrasound, so I headed there. A lot of the interns tried to get McClean's signature because he generally didn't ask too many questions and was more likely than the others to sign the form. The door of the ultrasound room was closed, and I stood with my ear against it trying to listen for voices, but I couldn't hear anything. I rapped gently on it and went inside. McClean was performing an ultrasound on someone and didn't turn around when

I went in. The nurse who was with him glared at me but didn't say anything. I went over to McClean and stood off to the side, behind his back. The ultrasound machine was blocking my view of whomever he was scanning – I could just see the bare skin of their abdomen, their legs, McClean's shoulder swaying rhythmically above the patient as he moved the probe across her body. It was quiet, almost peaceful in the room, and I understood why several of the interns had already decided they wanted to do radiology.

– Do you have something? McClean called out, and it took me a second to realize he was talking to me.

– Yes, I said, approaching him. It's a patient of Professor Lynch's. A woman who's lost a ton of weight, loads of abdominal pain, it's really bad.

– An actual ton? McClean said. Wow, that really is a mystery.

I was standing directly behind him, talking to the back of his head. Although he was one of the nicer radiologists, McClean could still be a prick. His manner was that of an old man even though he was probably only about forty. He wore dickie bows and immaculate striped shirts, sometimes even a waistcoat. He continued performing his ultrasound and didn't say anything else.

— We were wondering if it might be a lymphoma, I said.

— You guys always say that. Does Sharif even know what lymphoma is?

He asked the patient to breathe in and out.

— How long has she been in hospital? he asked me then.

— A few months, I said.

— Hold on, it's not that Therese woman is it? The one with anorexia? I read her last scan, it was one hundred per cent normal – why in God's name do you want to do another one on her? That's just a waste of everyone's time, including hers by the way.

The nurse was looking at me and then I realized that the patient on the table was also looking at me, following the back and forth with McClean.

– Breathe in again please, he said.

For a second I thought he was talking to me. The woman must have thought so too because he had to repeat the command. His voice had a wounded quality. You could appreciate its potential for bad temper. Now out, he said, and she did so eagerly. They repeated this a few times. I looked around the room. A couple of the wall monitors were on, and this is where all the light in the room was coming from.

– You're still here? McClean said to me over his shoulder.

– I thought you were thinking about it, I said.

He seemed to find this funny. Even the nurse smiled.

– Look, he said, why don't you go and talk to whoever is on CT? You might have more luck with them. But for what it's worth, I don't think that woman should have any more imaging. It's other help she needs.

I left the room and wandered down the corridor, holding on to the unsigned requisition form. The rota had said that Wilson was on CT, and there was no way he'd sign off on it for me, and he was going to be on CTs for the rest of the week. The whole thing was pointless, especially because I agreed with what McClean had said. A scan would do nothing for Therese. I put the form back in my pocket and left the department through the back door, which led on to the main link corridor. I heard my name and turned to see Stuart and Rosie. Stuart asked me was I headed to this thing, and it was only then that I noticed that the corridor was thronged with other staff and they all seemed to be headed in the one direction. It was the memorial service for Hanratty, Stuart said, did I not see the notices about it? They were up everywhere. Rosie didn't say anything. Stuart said he was shocked when he found out the news, absolutely shocked, God almighty it was such a tragedy, he had really liked Dr Hanratty, he was always so approachable, unlike certain people, and Rosie said ha, that's for sure. When we passed the turn-off that would have brought me back to the ward I didn't take it but instead continued on with the crowd, which was strung out almost the entire length of the corridor. We walked together in silence, or at least I was silent. Rosie and Stuart carried on a conversation that I couldn't make out, his mother was mentioned and she laughed and then she said something about her mother and he laughed. I told them that I didn't realize there were so many people working in the hospital, and seeing them all strung out along the length of the corridor was, I don't know, but I didn't finish the sentence. I guessed that the service was going to be in the chapel out the back of the hospital, and sure enough we went through the ambulance bay door on the other side of A & E. As we passed the burns unit the door opened and some of the nurses came out of it, probably on their way to the canteen, and looked surprised to see the procession of staff. I glanced down at where they had come from, but the momentum of the crowd pushed me forward and suddenly we were in the blustery sunny morning with the recent rain causing big puddles which darkened the hem of the scrubs belonging to the person walking in front of me. We filed into the chapel and quickly the seats were full and it was standing room only. The chapel was very bare, austere, I had never been in it before, and come to think of it I hadn't been inside any church in years. There were no paintings, or any of the other trappings of a church, no carvings of the crucified Christ, the blood dripping from his scalp, the nailed hands, the spear gash in his side. It was the bare bones of a church, the walls an off-grey, the ceiling yellowy. Many of the staff members who had gathered were familiar to me by sight, cleaners and porters, nurses, catering staff, as well as some of the ancillary people, dieticians, physios, OTs.

There was no sign of Hanratty's wife or children. It was also apparent that none of the consultants were there, and actually there were only a few doctors – me, Stuart and Rosie, and one or two others. The absence of the consultants gave the service a subversive feel, as if we had gathered to promote a threatening ideology. The priest started the proceedings abruptly and fairly whizzed through things. It wasn't a formal mass and it was not clear what its structure was. I was accustomed to seeing the priest on his travels around the hospital, where he was a quiet and good-humoured presence, quick to run out of a patient's room ahead of our ward round when we arrived there. Even if I was on my own, carrying my little foil tray and ready to take blood from the patient he was chatting to, he would finish what he was saying and get out of the way even though I never asked him to. But the chapel was his zone, and here he was different, more sure of himself, unequivocally in charge. He said that we should say a decade of the rosary for Dr Hanratty, and we joined him, the words coming back to me effortlessly after God knows how many years, and it was soothing and I would have been happy to go on chanting that meaningless chant for hours. Beside me, Stuart had his eyes tightly closed but was not speaking any of the words and it occurred to me that he was a Protestant. The priest gave a small homily, in which he asked us to pray for those colleagues among us who were struggling and walking with their own pain along their path, struggling with the burden of their existence, the job that they had been called to do. To help others when it didn't feel that that's what was happening. He paused for a second. The burden, he said again, of what they were carrying. Because it is a burden. Make no mistake about that. We are all human and we are only human. No matter what your badge says or whether you even have one, whether you're wearing a white coat or lying in bed with a drip going into your arm, we are all human and there is no difference between any of us. Humans looking after other humans. Doing our best. If there was anyone here who felt that they were in the darkness, then they should ask for help and they should not be afraid to do so, as God was always there to listen to them, and when he said those words he stopped and looked into the audience, and some of us looked back at him and some of us looked at the floor. For a few moments we were uncertain whether the ceremony had ended, but slowly a momentum developed to leave and we filed out of the chapel in silence. The air was colder and more over-cast than before, with a sky full of foreboding, the breeze laced with moisture. We re-entered the hospital via the ambulance bay and moved silently up the central corri-dor, the crowd thinning and dispersing as we went.

I met Stuart and Rosie later that evening in the res. We were on call and they were in the kitchen sitting beside each other at the long table. When I passed by the door on my way to one of the rooms to get changed they called out to me and I came back and stood at the doorway, my bag on my back. They were both already dressed in their scrubs.

— Are you OK man? Stuart asked me.

— Why? I said, but I knew what he was talking about. I was practically still shaking from the experience.

— Professor Lynch, he said.

— Stuart said it was horrible, Rosie said.

I tried not to look at them. Even though I had been expecting some grief from Sharif for not being able to arrange the scan for Therese it was a shock when Lynch showed up on the ward to have a go at me. He virtually never came on to the ward unless it was for the consultant round, and even that was only once a week. I can only imagine what Sharif must have been whispering into his ear about me while they stood beside each other all day operating on someone's oesophagus. Whatever it was, here was Lynch striding like a bull down the aisle of the ward.

— Where's the intern? he asked the ward sister.

She was as shocked as I was to see him on the ward, and she nodded in the direction of where I was sitting at the other end of the nurses' station entering lab results from the computer into the folder. Lynch stood in front of me and sized me up in silence. It was as if he was seeing me for the first time. He took a step towards me. For a second I thought he was going to get physical. I braced myself for the screaming fit that was about to erupt. He had come close enough that I would be able to feel the flecks of moisture on my face.

— I wanted to get a good look at you, he said, in case I ever come across you again. I've heard nothing but bad about you.

He paused again and leaned in further.

— Just in case our paths cross again.

His eyes narrowed and he leaned in another inch or two,

as if readying himself to squeeze as much vitriol into the words as possible. I was aware of everyone looking at us.

  – On an interview panel, Lynch said. Or any other
  fucking thing in life.

He stared at me for a long moment, then he tapped the side of his forehead and gave a little grin. Then he backed away, still tapping the side of his forehead like a maniac as if to say, I've got you in here now, I've got you in here and I never forget this sort of thing. Stuart's team were right beside us, they happened to be on the ward seeing a consult. Stuart's consultant was young and popular and he said hello to Lynch, but the older man glared at him and brushed past him and walked down the corridor and off the ward. Stuart looked at me, his face full of concern, just as it was now in the res.

  – No scheme for me then I guess, I said to him and
  Rosie, before turning away and heading to one of
  the on-call rooms to get changed.

It turned out to be another busy night and we decided to split the wards again, although later on when I came across Stuart and Rosie they seemed to be still going around together as a pair. I didn't mind and it didn't bother me being on my own, I even volunteered to cover the burns unit if they called. It was just after midnight when we met outside Sir Patrick Duns and we stood for a while chatting, comparing how the night was going for each of us, which wards were busier than others, which nurses were on, whether there were any sickies around the place. Stuart's pager went off and, laughing, he showed the number to me. It was the burns unit, which I had just volunteered to cover. Perfect timing, he said. I left Stuart and Rosie to go on to the adjacent Duns ward so that I could use the phone to call them. The burns unit answered straight away. The nurse told me they had a list of jobs compiled, so one trip should do it. It was mainly charting fluids, she said, but there was one review they wanted also, nothing urgent. When I came back out of Duns, Stuart and Rosie were gone and I made my way down to the ground level and along the link corridor. The closer I got to A & E the colder it got, as if the doors were constantly opening to let people in, though when I got all the way down there, A & E itself didn't seem too busy. As I stood at the front door to the burns unit waiting to be buzzed in, the ambulance bay across the way opened for the paramedics who were bringing someone in on a stretcher. The person was covered in blood and holding something up to their face. They had a neck brace on and the other arm was hanging limp by their side. It didn't look right and was no doubt in bits. The person seemed in a bad way and I couldn't imagine being the A & E doctor who would have to assess them and begin the process of repairing their broken body. Where would you even begin?

The burns unit door clicked open and I walked down the long corridor of the ward to the nurses' station. Two nurses wearing scrubs were sitting there and they greeted me in a friendly manner. They were very organized and had a list of things prepared of what they needed done. Everything was there already, I didn't have to go looking for anything. Sit, one of them said, indicating an empty chair beside them. They had even written in the fluid orders and specified how much potassium supplementation they needed, and they had written in the dates and times and all I had to do was sign my name. They sat beside me, putting each sheet in front of me, making sure I didn't miss anything, and we got through the pile very quickly, it was almost enjoyable. I knew what Lynda meant now when she spoke about the nurses down here. I wanted to ask them about her. It occurred to me that they may have heard from her. But we kept working away, the nurses putting one fluid sheet after another in front of me, and me signing them without paying too much attention. Afterwards they brought me over to one of the patient rooms, they wanted me to take a look at someone. We stood in the small anteroom adjacent to the patient's room and I was handed a gown and gloves to wear because of the infection risk. Poor little duck, one of the nurses said as she was pushing open the door. He's only sixteen. She turned to me and shook her head. Deep fat fryer, she said. The room was dark and the other nurse put on the small light above the bed, although this didn't project much. The bed complex was surrounded by monitors, and a large tube came out of the mattress, pulsing it with air. The room was very warm, and it was hard to make out any human form beneath the mound of wrapping and dressings, all covered in silver foil. There was extensive bandaging and a strong non-human smell of antiseptic, but beneath it the hint of something else, a tinge of the organic, open cavities, singed flesh. The monitors that surrounded the bed were beeping in a regular fashion, and although I only spent a brief moment looking at them and didn't fully understand the information they were displaying, they seemed happy, bleeping contentedly away in their alien language. I knew I would not have much to contribute but felt strangely comfortable in that knowledge – I would do my best. He seems a bit more settled now, one of the nurses said. He was having a lot of abdominal pain earlier. The three of us stood looking at the patient, and the steady rise and fall of the bedclothes. It was obvious that the patient was comfortable now, whatever the cause of his earlier pain, and was now sleeping soundly. False alarm, I guess, the nurse said. Here, she said, seeing as you're here, will you take a look at this? I followed her over to the other side of the bed. Do you think this is infected? She lifted up one of the teenager's bandages to reveal the Hickman catheter emerging out of his upper chest wall. She pointed at the exit site and it did seem a little red and tender. A small bubble of pus had gathered around it.

— We could try swabbing it, I said.

— We've sent a swab already, the other nurse said, but do you think we need to change his antibiotics?

— What's he on at the moment?

— Vanc and cipro.

— I'd say he's well covered from a Gram-positive point of view, I said, but you could check with the team in the morning, I wouldn't want to change anything until the sensitivities come back, especially if he's well otherwise.

The nurse seemed happy with this and we left the room, taking off our protective equipment in the small anteroom. We went back to the nurses' station. One of the nurses already had the chart out and sat next to me as I wrote a brief note. The other nurse headed off to check on something.

— Have you heard from Lynda? I asked the nurse beside me. I've tried ringing her a few times but it goes straight to her voice message. I hope she's OK.

— Oh she'll be grand, the nurse said, as long as she doesn't break her leg or something.

I must have given her a confused look because she stood up and removed a postcard from the noticeboard on the wall and put it down in front of me.

— The girls got this from her yesterday.

It was a picture of Mont Blanc, and on the other side a short message in Lynda's unmistakable slanted handwriting hoping that they weren't missing her too much and saying that she was really very busy altogether. And beside that she had drawn a little cartoon of a champagne bottle and a glass. Back to the slopes! she wrote.

   – Everyone I know who's gone skiing has come back with their leg in plaster, said the nurse.

I finished writing the note and thanked the nurses for their help and left the ward, pulling the door of the burns unit shut behind me. The ambulance bay doors opposite opened due to my presence and I could see out to the black night, which was as dense as outer space. The cold air invited me outside and I went briefly through the sentient doors. There was no breeze and not even the slightest moisture from any rain, and the night was a suspension of cold air on my skin. As I turned back to look at the lit-up emergency department – the large fluorescent sign, the bright waiting area, the parked ambulances docked to its hub – my arms and body felt incredibly light in the buoyant air, and, closing my eyes, I could as easily have been floating adrift in it, moving further and further away.

The rest of the night was OK. A steady stream of bleeps for another hour or so, but then things seemed to quieten down as if some agreement had been hammered out behind the scenes. Although I was tired I took my time getting back to the res. The last thing I wanted was to go to bed only to have to leave it again. I didn't run into Stuart or Rosie, and at a certain point I went to the res and sat for a long time in the kitchen lit by the gaudy fluorescence of the buzzing lights above my head.

Lynda was back at work on Friday, just in time for what was to be our final night on call together. I got a glimpse of her at some point during the day through the doors of the burns unit. The blonde head of her, she was already dressed in her scrubs for the coming night. She turned to look in my direction and I pulled my head away just in time. When I looked back she was still staring my way and I had no choice but to wave at her. I hurried away to radiology to arrange scans, or to the vascular lab for a Doppler, or to microbiology to drop off blood cultures, or to theatre or pathology, or to put in a line or do a blood gas on someone or quickly admit somebody from the day unit or put in a catheter or get a work cert for one of the discharges or look for someone's long-lost X-ray packet in the bowels of the archive room. In other words, it was a fairly typical day, with my pager going off every minute, or even several times a minute, like a barometer which reflected how busy the hospital was, how alert it was in its surveillance of me, and also how angry and impatient it was, demanding to know why I was here and not there, doing this and not that, reminding me that I was useless and inept and wholly inefficient, and there was barely a moment's respite from any of this, from one end of the day to the other.

Sharif, though, was in eerily good humour. Lynch had broken his ankle, which meant that he wouldn't be around for the next few weeks, possibly even a couple of months. Instantly the spectre of him both vanished and, at the same time, could be now fully appreciated, how overshadowing it was, the magnitude of it, the evil spirit that diffused out of it, and which we could see clearly had been hanging around us and stalking us. The rumours were flying about how Lynch had sustained the fracture. All sorts of stuff. It was cancer of the bone and he was riddled. Or he did it climbing out of a window, on some amorous mission. Or he had fallen out of bed in the middle of the night and wasn't found until the next day, half rigid with hypothermia. One of the more optimistic strands of speculation had it that this would bring him up to his retirement and we'd never have to set eyes on the fucker again. Or alternatively, went another strand of speculation, he'd be back by Friday worse than ever just to spite us, and this I found easiest to visualize. Regardless, it was clear on the ward round that the relief of Lynch's absence had seeped into every pore of Sharif's skin. He was all charm and jokes, as relaxed as I had ever seen him, gently poking fun at the SHOs. This was when

I found out they were a couple. Is she like this at home? Sharif asked the male SHO. Unfortunately yes, was the reply, and she jokingly thumped him on the arm, both annoyed and pretending to be annoyed. Sharif and the male SHO laughed. The ward round stretched on for over an hour and Sharif seemed in no rush to get to the operating room – he spent some time chatting with the patients, and even asked one man what he did for a living. At the end, when we were going over the list of jobs, he seemed fairly relaxed about things.

- See if you can get a scan, he said in relation to one of the new admissions. Who's on CT this week?

- Wilson, I said.

Sharif puffed out his cheeks.

- That'll be tough, he said. Well, at least get him an ultrasound. Better that than nothing.

He didn't say anything about the previous Friday and the business of Therese's scan. Obviously we didn't round on her, she was back to not existing again. When I went to take her bloods she barely said a word, and she didn't ask me any of her usual questions about what tests

174

were planned or what was in store for her. It occurred to me that she was annoyed with me for not being able to arrange the scan for her and transfer her to the medics like I had promised. But that wasn't it, because as I was tidying up she said she was sorry. I barely heard her she said it so quietly. I asked her what for. She said she'd heard I got in trouble with Lynch over it. It was her stupid fault she said. She didn't know what was wrong with her. Maybe they were right. Maybe it was all in her head. She wanted to go home. She was leaning on her arm, her bony fingers splayed against the white sheet. They were long and elegant like those of a concert pianist and I got a glimpse of a whole other life for her, one that never got a chance to happen, but that easily could have. She looked downwards and it was easy to imagine that any other person would have been crying. But she was the type of person who was beyond that, the tears had dried out of her, evaporated long ago during the years of her childhood, whatever miseries she had endured. I couldn't imagine a single moment of happiness for her in her life. I told her I'd check who was on CT next week and you never know, but more than likely it wouldn't happen this week.

She continued looking downwards at her splayed hand.

– We'll get to the bottom of it, I said, I promise.

She looked at me and seemed happy with what I had said despite the fact that neither of us believed it to be true.

I didn't catch up with Lynda until later that evening. It must have been almost nine by the time I met her in the res. She'd been hauled into theatre late in the afternoon and was only now getting out. Luckily it was quiet around the place and we had been able to manage without her. Apparently her consultant wanted to show her how to suture properly before she left the team. Before those general surgeons get their clutches on you, she had said to Lynda. In her consultant's opinion, the general surgeons were nothing more than butchers. Ham-fisted. Whenever they were involved you could just forget about cosmesis altogether.

– Don't tell Sharif she said that, I said, you'll start a war.

– I think she was talking about the older ones, Lynda said. The likes of Lynch and Bailey. Sharif's got good technique actually.

She went on to say that she had run into Sharif earlier.

Apparently he had also invited her into theatre that afternoon, to scrub in for one of the long cases, but she couldn't make it. She acted as if this was all a big hassle, but it was obvious that they were chasing after her. The Scheme had a few different tracks to it and the prospective candidates had to rank their preferences. The consultants all wanted Lynda on their rotations. We were in the kitchen of the res, and she was making herself tea. She turned around then and switched off the kettle before it had finished.

— By the way, she said back to me, did you hear about Lynch?

— Yes, I said, his ankle.

— He's in Colles ward, she said.

I hadn't heard that.

— Jesus, I hope I'm not called to put a line into him, I said.

— It's not that I'd be worried about if I was you, she said.

She turned around, smiling.

— What? I said, but she just stood there smiling.

— You'd better be hoping he doesn't need a urinary catheter, she then said, turning away.

I stared over at her, the straight back of her as she made her tea. She turned back to me again and started laughing at the expression on my face. She held out her thumb and forefinger.

— We'd have to go looking for it, she said, and we both laughed.

Stuart and Rosie came into the kitchen. They said hello to Lynda and stood over me. I had a Chinese open in front of me and felt self-conscious about it because I hadn't bothered to ask if they wanted one. I knew by now they would be doing their own thing. Rosie wasn't even supposed to be on call. She'd swapped with the geriatric intern who was rostered for that night, but the geri's call was an absolute joke, she said, so she was happy to help us. After standing for a second, Stuart sat down opposite me and Rosie took the seat next to him. Lynda came over and joined us, but immediately took out her pager and started fiddling with it. She said the time on it was wrong all year and she was determined to finally fix it. We watched her in silence as she fiddled with it. It was hard to believe that this was going to be our last night on call together. The following week we were due to change rotations and both Lynda and Stuart were heading to different parts of the country, while I would be moving to ENT. I had forgotten about this until Sharif mentioned it earlier. He asked me what I was doing next, and I stared back at him mutely. What rotation? he said, but then he didn't wait for the answer. He wanted to know about the next intern they'd be getting, and I told him she was excellent, there would be no worries there. His eyes narrowed and he looked at me. What do you want to do anyway? he said. Long term? You mean you don't think I should go for The Scheme? I said. We both laughed. Seriously, he said, and he was looking at me in a genuinely curious fashion. Don't tell me you're going to be a fanny doctor? Or work in the nut house maybe? In Sharif's view, all of the medical specialties could be boiled down to one or other of these two categories. But then he adopted what for him was a philosophical tone. Look man, he said, it's not for everyone, this surgery business. I would have liked to have said something cutting back to him. That surgeons were just plumbers at the end of the day, technicians

179

who didn't understand what they were dealing with most of the time. Whatever piece of the body they happened to be removing or repairing, the physiology of it, what was a total mystery to the likes of Sharif, or would be if he ever stopped to think about it for a moment. But I didn't say any of that, and he took out his little notebook and started flicking through it, having already moved on from our conversation.

Lynda was still fiddling away with her pager, and for a while we watched her, or certainly I did. She was utterly absorbed by what she was doing.

– Which reminds me, Lynda, Stuart said to her, and she seemed relieved to have an excuse to put the pager down.

He asked her had she put in her application for The Scheme yet and would she mind taking a look at his if she got a chance later on? Lynda looked back at him for a moment, the surprise not particularly evident on her face, except perhaps in the way she continued to just stare at him without answering.

– The surgical scheme? she said then.

– Yeah, he replied. Psychiatry's not for me I don't think.

Lynda couldn't resist smiling. She looked at me, then back at Stuart.

  – They're not due yet, she said, it's only the
  Expression of Interest they want, for numbers.
  But sure, she said, I'll take a look.

Stuart thanked her. She took up her pager again and it went off while she was still holding it in her hands. Bennetts, she said, checking the number. Straight away Stuart volunteered to head over there. Sure I've just come from there, he said. In any case, he was feeling antsy, he said, so he might go and do a quick sweep of the wards. We could stay here and finish our tea, he said, he'd call us if it got busy around the place. Rosie said she'd tag along with him. After they had gone Lynda gave me a look and I said, I know, I know. She started laughing. What the . . .? she said and laughed again. I know, I said again. We could hear Stuart whistling as he headed down the corridor of the res. He was a good strong whistler, I'd noticed that before about him, especially at night the way the acoustics worked. It was just me and Lynda again on our own in the kitchen. I got up and made a

coffee and then sat down across from her, where Stuart
had been sitting.

   — So, skiing? I said to her.

   — What's wrong with that?

   — I thought you were sick.

   — Sick? No, holidays. We got a last-minute deal and
I told admin to sort it out. Why, was it busy here?

   — The usual.

She had taken her pager in hand again and was working
on it. She was nothing if not obsessive about things, even
the smallest task.

   — So it wasn't anything to do with what happened?
I asked her.

   — What do you mean?

   — That African patient, I said. You know, Jesus?

   — Why, what's that got to do with anything?

— The fact that he died after the marrow.

She looked up from the pager to me. I was now staring directly into the fury of her pale green eyes.

— Is that what people are saying? Excuse me but I did everything there. That poor guy was in a full-on haemorrhagic state. He was bleeding out of his ears practically. At least I was trying to help him. Why, what were people saying?

— No, I said. Nobody's saying anything. I was just wondering.

— They'd just left him there, he was spiking up to forty. They had him on some Augmentin. Yeah he bled from the marrow, but he was bleeding internally as well. Probably into the lungs too, which is what killed him. By then he was too unstable to get down to the scanner.

She was quiet then, thinking.

— It was that fucker Donoghue, wasn't it? I knew he'd put the whole thing on me. He tried everything not to have to come in. And then when he did

183

eventually come in it was too late and he was focusing on the wrong thing. He started shouting at me. Typical male. He lost the head altogether, it was like dealing with a toddler. The stench of alcohol on his breath as well. Bastard.

She got up to make another coffee. The kettle boiled and it was another minute before she sat down opposite me again. Neither of us spoke for a while. Then I told her about Hanratty, but my tone was all wrong and it was as if I was telling her about some piece of gossip. She didn't say anything, and the news didn't seem to have any effect on her. She drank her coffee. She took up her pager but put it down in frustration after fiddling with it for a while.

 — Where did he do it? she asked. Hanratty.

 — The Amsterdam Hotel, I said. You know, the place near the airport? Apparently, anyway. They didn't make an announcement about it.

 — God, she said, I saw that place when we were headed skiing. It looked like the most depressing place on earth.

For some reason I laughed. I was familiar with it also. Weeks earlier I had come close to staying there. It was on one of the post-call days. I'd come home to find that my housemates were having a party. It was the last thing I wanted, the floor was heaving with the sound of music and conversation, so I got into my car and started to drive. I got caught up in relentless traffic that barely seemed to be moving an inch. I passed the hotel and, exhausted, considered checking in for the night. I even went as far as to pull into the empty car park, but I ended up not staying there and didn't even get out of the car. An image came to me of the place surrounded by wasteland, you could only imagine what the rooms were like, the carpet, the furniture that seemed to be from the seventies, a desk that nobody ever sat at, a pen which nobody ever used. There was a big desperate banner on the side of the building, advertising it as a vision of luxury, what must then come as such a disappointment.

My pager went off and it was Private 1. Lynda said she'd come with me. I didn't bother calling the number back because the ward itself was right next to the res. We stood up and left the kitchen and exited through the link corridor, which was in total darkness as usual, and freezing cold, a noticeable breeze coming through some gap in the flimsy wall. My pager went off again, as did

Lynda's shortly after. The same number for both of us. We were spotted from a distance as soon as we set foot on the ward.

— Here they are now Marie, a voice shouted out from somewhere.

The nurse appeared out of one of the side rooms and hurried towards us. You could tell straight away that she was in a real panic.

— It's Room 4, she said. We got him tonight, back from theatre. He's in a bad way, trying to climb over the rails. He's not right, he's going absolutely ape in there.

The nurse was talking only to me, completely ignoring Lynda, which I could tell she found amusing. She stood to one side with her hands in her pockets. Private 1 was renowned for not being able to cope. Acopic was the term we used about them. Generally the patients they had were totally fine, recovering from various elective procedures, varicose veins or having their tonsils out. The minute any of them ran into trouble the nurses panicked. More than likely this was another of these situations.

– What are his obs? Lynda said, impatient with this nurse, who seemed to be noticing Lynda now for the first time.

– Here, I have them written down, the nurse said, and she stuck out her arm towards us, pen marks showing on the back of her hand.

– Is that a seven or a one? Lynda said, trying not to laugh.

The nurse pulled her hand back and stared down at it.

– I think it's a seven, she said.

– What about the O2 sats? Lynda asked her.

– I don't know, couldn't get them. He was in such a rage.

Room 4 was directly across from the nurses' station and we went into it. There was a strange atmosphere in the room that could be immediately appreciated even as we were going through the door. A spirit of rage, pure aggression. I was shocked to see Professor Lynch sitting in the bed. He was dishevelled, wearing pyjamas, but the front of the jacket was open and the thick dark tangle of his chest hair was visible. I turned around and left the room. Lynda was behind me but hadn't entered the room yet.

— It's fucking Lynch, I said. I thought you said he was in Colles.

She stood for a second.

— That's what I was told, she said. It makes sense though. They wouldn't put a consultant in Colles.

She walked past me into the room. I followed her and we stood at the end of the bed. Lynch was staring at us like a wild animal. You could hear his breathing, a low purring. He didn't recognize me, but that was just the start of it. You could tell he was totally delirious. His body was tense, like a creature that had been fatally wounded and was ready to fight tooth and nail to the death. His arms were bleeding from where he'd pulled out the IV lines and scratched at the bandages with his nails. One of his ankles was in a fresh cast. His pyjamas were soaked through and the white bed sheet was stained dark red from a small pool of blood. I couldn't bring myself to go near him. Lynda went through the motions of introducing herself and was pleasant with him, but kept her distance, her eyes scanning him from all angles as she spoke gently to him. He flinched when she touched him lightly on his arm. It was obvious that he wasn't going to let her do anything else. She stood back from him then and observed him. I couldn't see beyond the intensity of his eyes staring at me. Lynda walked past me and I followed her out of the room.

– He's delirious, she said. We'll have to give him an antipsychotic before we can do anything to him.

She was already up talking to the nurse standing by the drug trolley, and I followed them into the treatment room, where the nurse unlocked the drugs cabinet at Lynda's instruction. Lynda searched inside for the halo-peridol and asked me to get an insulin syringe. I did as she asked, and she drew some up then marched back to Lynch's room. He had one leg over the side rails of the bed. We stood for a second, Lynda directing the nurse with her eyes where to stand. Me and the three nurses were in position around the bed.

– Now. Quick, grab him, she said.

We descended on him and at first he didn't utter a sound. I pushed him over and leaned on his shoulder. Then the shouting started and he roared with naked fury. Lynda took the cap off the syringe and quickly jabbed the needle into his upper arm. She re-capped the needle and joined us in putting her weight on him, at the same time rubbing the area where she had injected to make sure it was absorbed. Lynch shouted and shunted his body around – he was unbelievably strong. Several times he broke free, but we were able to get on top of him and keep him from hurting himself. One of the nurses was hit in the face by his swinging fist. She stepped away, momentarily stunned, before rejoining the struggle. An age passed before anything happened. I asked Lynda should we give him another dose, but shortly after that we felt his resistance lessen, and then his breathing deepened and he was asleep, even letting out a few snores. We stood around the bed looking at him.

– Let's get a set of obs on him, I said.

The nurse went out to get the blood pressure machine. Lynda and I stood looking at him, both noticing the same things.

– He's tachypnoeic isn't he? I said.

The nurse returned and we watched as she did the obs.

– Ninety over sixty, she said.

– Should we be calling the crash team? I said.

– What good would that do? He's got a pulse and a BP.

– Right, I said, let's get to work on him then.

Lynda marched out of the room, and I followed her to the treatment room and without saying anything we started to get everything ready. Lynda drew up the anti-biotics and I got the various items needed to take bloods and cultures and put in a line.

– Is he allergic to anything? she asked me.

– How should I know? I said. I only work for him.

– I meant check his chart, she said.

On our way back I pulled his notes from the chart trol-ley. He wasn't allergic to anything. On the demographics page of the chart I lingered on some of the details. It was so odd to see them. His first name was listed as Thomas Patrick. I saw his birth date and calculated that he was sixty-four. His next of kin was down as his wife Joan. He was Roman Catholic. He lived on Shrewsbury Road. He had Vhi Plan B. Lynda called my name and I went into the room.

— Can you put the line in please? A trace of irritation in her voice.

I put two lines into him, one in each arm, both large bore just in case, 16 gauge. There was no problem with either of them, they went right in, no doubt helped by the fact that his veins were engorged, the infected blood coursing through them. I also did all the bloods via the second cannula and then, separately, the blood cultures. The nurses strapped both IVs heavily. If he woke he'd have to gnaw at them with his teeth to get at them. But there was no sign of that – he was in a deep sleep. Lynda had left the room, but now appeared pushing a trolley. I saw she had set up to catheterize him.

— Do you want to do the honours? she said.

We worked quickly and the catheter was in in no time. It wasn't strange putting it in, even when we pulled down his pyjama bottoms and cleaned the groin area with Betadine. The bag quickly filled with urine, and it was clear that he had been in retention on top of everything else.

— Fucking orthopods, Lynda said. All they care about is hammering their nails into the bone.

She took off her gloves and put the rubbish in a yellow bag and tied it. She stood thinking for a few moments.

— We should put him on Clexane, she said. He's a sitting duck for a clot.

I agreed and, picking up the kardex, charted it. Then we stood looking at him. There was literally nothing else we could do for him. Lynda went out to write the note in the chart. As she did so, I leaned on the nurses' station looking down at her. She looked tired.

— Here, give me your bleep, I said. Why don't you go and get some sleep?

She paused to look at me.

— There's no point in the pair of us being up, I said. I feel fine. Plus I might just hang here a bit longer, to make sure things have stabilized.

Lynda seemed to accept this and handed over her bleep. When she finished her note she got up and headed back to the res. I took her place at the nurses' station and sat for a while not doing anything in particular. The nurses were chatting among themselves, deciding on which break each of them would take, first or second. But they were more relaxed now and their relief was palpable. I felt that if they asked me to do something it would be no problem, but they left me alone. After a while I got up and went back to check on Lynch. The earlier atmosphere in the room had vanished, the raw aggression replaced by something peaceful, the sound of his sleep. I stood for a while looking at him, counting his breaths even though I knew the rate was normal. It struck me that I was exhausted, or maybe it was just my relief that the thing was done, and these feelings were indistinguishable from each other, relief that the task was accomplished, but either way it was a pleasant exhaustion, something we had become familiar with during the last few months, though we never spoke about it, what now and again the night gave back in place of sleep, and it was a fine thing, a form of acceptance for everything we were able to do and everything we were not able to do.

One of the nurses came into the room and, whispering, asked me if I wouldn't mind going into Room 9. She wouldn't have called me about it, she said, and there was nothing I could do about it, but since I was here on the ward already, perhaps I could just pop in to them. A woman who was actively dying. Cheyne stoking, she said. The family were there, they were very nice, and it would look good if a doctor went in to reassure them that things were happening the way they were supposed to. Obviously there was nothing I could do, she said again, but maybe go in, it would mean a lot to them. No problem I said, and she led me down the corridor and into the room after rapping very lightly on the door. The room was surprisingly crowded, with people of different ages, even relatively young children. On the bed was a woman who was in the last stages, her breathing had entered that unnatural rhythm. But her face was very peaceful, as if it had disconnected entirely from her body. I nodded at the family and stood for a few seconds looking at the woman, in awe of what was happening to her, a process that was not of this world but a glimpse into another one. The family were watching me now and I looked back at them as kindly as I could. After a while I stepped forward, uncoiling my stethoscope. I listened to the woman's lungs and looked into her mouth with my pen torch. It was no easy thing to pry open the jaws. I couldn't really hear anything in the lungs on account of the loud grunting, and the mouth itself was filled with the blackness that had already seeped into her body. I pressed lightly on her stomach, which was soft. I put my stethoscope away and turned to face the family. I stepped forward, composed, like an actor facing an audience bathed in half-light. She seems comfortable, I said, but if they had any concerns during the night to let the nurses know, there was plenty we could do and that's why we were here. And please, I said, feel free to talk to her, their mother, their wife, their grandmother, it was possible she might hear them at some level, and this might provide comfort to her. Several of them whispered their thanks and I walked calmly out of the room. The nurse was waiting for me in the corridor. She thanked me and I said no problem, I didn't really do anything. No, she said, it would have meant a lot to them. I left the ward and walked around the adjacent area of the hospital, a little aimlessly and at no great pace, but I didn't get any more bleeps and already the night was nearly over. After a while I decided to head back to the res, where I sat in the kitchen. At a certain point I went to bed. There were only a few more bleeps during the night, nothing urgent, and I must have slept. When I woke sunlight was streaming through the window. I showered and had some coffee and toast with the others and together we waited for the day interns to come in so that we could hand over to them. Then we left the res and headed out into the world, which was filled with a harsh and heatless sun. The grass sparkled with dew. I left Stuart and Lynda by the visitors' car park, which was almost completely empty, and we went our separate ways.

Acknowledgements

I WANT TO thank the following people: Bella Lacey, and everyone at Granta; Mandy Woods; Faith O'Grady; Lisa Bellamy, Peter Krass and Cynthia Weiner of The Writers Studio in New York for setting me on the road; and much earlier than this, Sydney Peck. I would like to thank my parents – Vincent and Pauline Duffy – for everything, and my sister and brother, Eleanor Ward and Garrett Duffy, for all their support; and lastly, my partner in life, friend and first reader, Naomi Taitz Duffy, also for everything.

TEN DAYS

'A terrific novel' William Boyd

'Quietly wonderful' *Sunday Times*

———————————

Set across the High Holy Days of Rosh Hashanah and Yom Kippur, *Ten Days* is a tender, nuanced and beautifully crafted story of a father's reckoning with his daughter and a profound, compelling meditation on family, time and the bonds of marriage.

Wolf travels to New York with his daughter to scatter the ashes of his recently estranged wife, Miriam. Buffeted by the loss, his fraught relationship with his daughter and the antagonism of Miriam's conservative Jewish family, Wolf is also coming to terms with a burgeoning concern of his own: growing dislocations in his mind, and the hollowing out of his memories.

———————————

'An absolutely beautiful book about time and mortality, love and memory, in which heartbreaking sadness and dry humour are held in exquisite tension' Carys Davies

'Sensitive and unexpected ... devastating. Duffy's skilful pacing reveals the truth piece by piece' *Irish Times*

'Delicately textured ... [Duffy] generates a steady supply of uneasy comedy as well as poignancy' *Daily Mail*